"I think this one's for you," he said, and handed it over.

She didn't drop it.

To her eternal credit—and thinking back later she was very, very proud of herself—she took the baby, just like the professional she was. Midwife receiving a baby at handover. She gathered her as she'd gather any infant she didn't know; any child when she didn't know its history. Taking care to handle her lightly with no pressure on anywhere that might hurt. Cradling her and holding her instinctively against her body, giving warmth as she'd give warmth to any tiny creature.

But for the moment her eyes were all on Blake.

He looked almost forbidding. Looming in her doorway, six feet two or three, wide shoulders, dark, dark eyes made even darker by the faint glow of moonlight, deep, black hair, a shadowy figure.

Tall, dark and dangerous....

Dear Reader,

This year our family farm is to be leased out as my brother retires from farming. One of the next generation may well decide farming's the life for them, but it needs to be a decision they make in the future, when the time's right for them. Thus, for now, more than a hundred years of farming history is pausing.

For me this is a sadness. Although I've long left behind the reality of twice daily milking, our family farm has never lost its power, its warmth, its pull. Happily though, I can still disappear into my farming community in my books.

As you may have read in my introduction to *Mardie and the City Surgeon,* recently the farm was flooded. At midnight a neighbor rang my brother to say the river had broken its banks, and a paddock full of calves was disappearing underwater. My brother and sister-in-law thus spent the night in their kids' ancient canoe, saving every one of their calves.

The story was a fun one, with a happy ending, and with the half-grown calves reacting like excited kids when they were finally rescued. The story made me smile—and as always it made me think What if? What if I threw my city surgeon hero into such a scene? What if my heroine had to depend on him? What if...what if I even threw a wounded baby into the mix?

I love my writing, where reality and fantasy can mingle to become pure fun. As you read this, however, know that the calves are real, the happy ending true and each rescued calf is now a safe and cared for member of a magnificent herd. Our farm, our heritage stays alive, in the hearts of every one of our family members, and hopefully in the warmth and fun my writing enables me to share.

Warm wishes,

from a bit of an emotional Marion

THE SURGEON'S DOORSTEP BABY

Marion Lennox

HARLEQUIN®

entertain, enrich, inspire™

Recycling programs
for this product may
not exist in your area.

ISBN-13: 978-0-373-06863-0

THE SURGEON'S DOORSTEP BABY

First North American Publication 2013

Copyright © 2013 by Marion Lennox

www.Harlequin.com

Printed in U.S.A.

**These books are also available in ebook format
from www.Harlequin.com.**

To Cobrico. To Mayfield. To my beloved family
who form the bedrock of who I am.

CHAPTER ONE

As CHIEF orthopaedic surgeon for one of Sydney's most prestigious teaching hospitals, Blake Samford was used to being woken in the middle of the night for emergencies.

Right now, however, he was recuperating at his father's farm, two hundred miles from Sydney.

He wasn't expecting an emergency.

He wasn't expecting a baby.

Maggie Tilden loved lying in the dark, listening to rain on the corrugated-iron roof. She especially liked lying alone to listen.

She had a whole king-sized bed to herself. Hers, all hers. She'd been renting this apartment—a section of the grandest homestead in Corella Valley—for six months now, and she was savouring every silent moment of it.

Oh, she loved being free. She loved being here. The elements could throw what they liked at her; she was gloriously happy. She wriggled her toes luxuriously against her cotton sheets and thought, Bring it on, let it rain.

She wasn't even worried about the floods.

This afternoon the bridge had been deemed unsafe. Debris from the flooded country to the north was being slammed against the ancient timbers, and the authorities were worried the whole thing would go. As of that afternoon, the bridge was roped off and the entire valley was isolated.

Residents had been advised to evacuate and many had, but a lot of the old-time farmers wouldn't move if you put a bulldozer under them. They'd seen floods before. They'd stocked up with provisions, they'd made sure their stock was on high ground and they were sitting it out.

Maggie was doing the same.

A clap of thunder split the night and Tip, the younger Border collie, whined and edged closer to the bed.

'It's okay, guys,' she told them, as the ancient Blackie moved in for comfort as well. 'We're safe and dry, and we have a whole month's supply of dog food. What else could we want?'

And then she paused.

Over the sound of the driving rain she could hear a car. Gunned, fast. Driving over the bridge?

It must have gone right around the roadblock.

Were they crazy? The volume of water powering down the valley was a risk all by itself. There were huge warning signs saying the bridge was unsafe.

But the bridge was still intact, and the car made it without mishap. She heard the change in noise as it reached the bitumen on this side, and she relaxed, expecting the car's noise to fade as it headed inland.

But it didn't. She heard it turn into her driveway—okay, not hers, but the driveway of the Corella View Homestead.

If the car had come from this side of the river she'd be out of bed straight away, expecting drama. As district nurse, she was the only person with medical training on this side of the river—but the car had come from the other side, where there was a hospital and decent medical help.

She'd also be worrying about her brother. Pete was in the middle of teenage rebellion, and lately he'd been hanging out with some dubious mates. The way that car was being driven…danger didn't begin to describe it.

But this was someone from the other side. Not Pete. Not a medical emergency. Regardless, she swung her feet out of bed and reached for her robe.

And then she paused.

Maybe this was a visitor for her landlord.

A visitor at midnight?

Who knew? She hardly knew her landlord.

Blake Samford was the only son of the local squattocracy—squattocracies being the slang term for families who'd been granted huge tracts of land when Australia had first been opened to settlers and had steadily increased their fortunes since. The Corella Valley holding was impressive, but deserted. Blake had lived here as a baby but his mother had taken him away when he was six. The district had hardly seen him since.

This, however, was his longest visit for years. He'd arrived three days ago. He was getting over appendicitis, he'd told her, taking the opportunity to get the farm ready for sale. His father had been dead for six months. It was time to sell.

She'd warned him the river was rising. He'd shrugged.

'If I'm trapped, I might as well be truly trapped.'

If he was having visitors at midnight, they'd be trapped with him.

Maybe it's a woman, she thought, sinking back into bed as the car stopped and footsteps headed for Blake's side of the house—the grand entrance. Maybe he'd decided if he was to be trapped he needed company. Was this a woman ready to risk all to reach her lover?

Who knew? Who knew anything about Blake Samford?

Blake was a local yet not a local. She'd seen him sporadically as a kid—making compulsory access visits to his bully of a father, the locals thought—but as far as she knew he hadn't come near when his father had been ill. Given his father's reputation, no one blamed him. Finally she'd met him at the funeral.

She'd gone to the funeral because she'd been making daily medical checks on the old man for the last few months of his life. His reputation had been appalling, but he'd loved his dogs so she'd tried to convince herself he hadn't been all bad. Also, she'd needed to talk to his son about the dogs. And her idea.

She hadn't even been certain Blake would come but he'd been there— Blake Samford, all grown up. And stunning. The old ladies whispered that he'd inherited his mother's looks. Maggie had never known his mother, but she was definitely impressed by the guy's appearance—strong, dark, riveting. But not friendly. He'd stood aloof from the few locals present, expressionless, looking as if he was there simply to get things over with.

She could understand that. With Bob Samford as a father, it had been a wonder he'd been there at all.

But Maggie had an idea that needed his agreement. It had taken courage to approach him when the service had ended, to hand over her references and ask him about the housekeeper's apartment at the back of the homestead. To offer to keep an eye on the place as well as continuing caring for the dogs his dad had loved. Harold Stubbs, the next-door landowner, had been looking after Bob's cattle. The cattle still needed to be there to keep the grass down, but Harold was getting too old to take care of two herds plus the house and the dogs. Until Blake sold, would he like a caretaker?

Three days later a rental contract had arrived. She'd moved in but she hadn't heard from him since.

Until now. He was home to put the place on the market.

She'd expected nothing less. She knew it'd be sold eventually and she was trying to come up with alternative accommodation. She did *not* want to go home.

But right now her attention was all on the stupidity of his visitors driving over the bridge. Were they out of their minds?

She was tempted to pull back the drapes and look.

She heard heavy footsteps running across the veranda, and the knocker sounded so loudly it reverberated right through the house. The dogs went crazy. She hauled them back from the door, but as she did she heard the footsteps recede back across the veranda, back down the steps.

The car's motor hadn't been cut. A car door

slammed, the engine was gunned—and it headed off the way it had come.

She held her breath as it rumbled back across the bridge. Reaching the other side. Safe.

Gone.

What on earth…?

Kids, playing the fool?

It was not her business. It was Blake's business, she told herself. He was home now and she was only caring for her little bit of the house.

Hers. Until Blake sold the house.

It didn't matter. For now it was hers, and she was soaking up every minute of it.

She snuggled back down under the covers—alone.

If there was one thing Maggie Tilden craved above everything else, it was being alone.

Bliss.

On the other side of the wall, Blake was listening, too. He heard the car roar over the bridge. He heard the thumps on his front door, the running footsteps of someone leaving in a hurry, and the car retreating back over the bridge.

He also thought whoever it was must be crazy.

He and his tenant—Maggie Tilden—had inspected the bridge yesterday. The storm water had been pounding the aged timbers; things were being swept fast downstream—logs, debris, some of it big. It was battering the piles.

'If you want to get out, you should go now,' Maggie had said. 'The authorities are about to close it.'

Did it matter? He'd been ordered to take three weeks off work to recuperate from appendicitis. He needed to sort his father's possessions, so what difference did it make if he was stranded while he did it?

'It's up to you,' Maggie had said, as if she didn't mind either way, and she'd headed back to her part of the house with his father's dogs.

She kept to herself, for which he was profoundly grateful, but now... A knock at midnight. A car going back and forth over the bridge.

Was this some friend of hers, playing the fool? Leaving something for her at the wrong door?

Whoever they were, they'd gone.

On Maggie's side of the house he'd heard the dogs go crazy. He imagined her settling them. Part of him expected her to come across to check what had just happened.

She didn't.

Forget it, he told himself. Go back to bed.

Or open the door and make sure nothing had been left?

The knock still resonated. It had been loud, urgent, demanding attention.

Okay, check.

He headed for the front door, stepped outside and came close to falling over a bundle. Pink, soft...

He stooped and tugged back a fold of pink blanket.

A thick thatch of black hair. A tiny, rosebud mouth. Snub nose. Huge dark eyes that stared upwards, struggling to focus.

A tiny baby. Three weeks at most, he thought, stunned.

Lying on his doorstep.

He scooped the infant up without thinking, staring out into the night rather than down at the baby, willing the car to be still there, willing there to be some sort of answer.

The bundle was warm—and moist. And alive.

A baby...

He had nothing to do with babies. Yeah, okay, he'd treated babies during medical training. He'd done the basic paediatric stuff, but he'd been an orthopaedic surgeon for years now, and babies hardly came into his orbit.

A baby was in his orbit now. In his arms.

He stared down at the baby, and wide eyes stared back.

A memory stabbed back. A long time ago. Thirty or more years? Here, in this hall.

A woman with a baby, placing the baby by the

door in its carry basket, pointing at Blake and saying, 'I've brought the kid his baby sister.'

After that, his memory blurred. He remembered his father yelling, and his mother screaming invective at his father and at the woman. He remembered the strange woman being almost hysterical.

He'd been six years old. While the grown-ups had yelled, he'd sidled over and looked at the baby it seemed everyone was yelling about. She'd been crying, but none of the grown-ups had noticed.

A baby sister?

He shook himself. That had been the night his mother had found out about his father's lover. He'd never seen either the woman or her baby again.

This baby was nothing to do with his history. Why was he thinking of it now?

He should call the police. He should report an abandoned baby.

Who looked like a baby he'd seen a long time ago?

And then he thought of Maggie, his tenant, and he remembered the references she'd given him.

She was the district nurse and she was also a midwife.

The relief that surged over him was almost overwhelming. This was nothing to do with him. Of course it wasn't. The whole valley knew Mag-

gie's job. If a woman wanted to abandon an un-
wanted child, what better way than dump it on
a woman you knew could look after it? Maybe
Maggie had even cared for the mother during her
pregnancy.

'Hey,' he said, relaxing, even holding the baby
a little tighter now he knew what he was dealing
with. The child seemed to be staring straight up
at him now, dark eyes wondering. 'You've come
to the wrong door. Okay, I know you're in trouble
but you *have* come to the right place—just one
door down. Hold on a minute and we'll take you
to someone who knows babies. To someone who
hopefully will take responsibility for getting you
out of this mess.'

Maggie was snuggling back down under the duvet
when someone knocked on *her* door and the dogs
went nuts again.

What? What now?

She'd worked hard today. She'd set up the entire
clinic, moving emergency gear from the hospital
over the river, trying to get everything organised
before the bridge closed. As well as that, she'd
made prenatal checks of women on farms that
were so wet right now that every able body was
moving stock and if Maggie wanted her pregnant
ladies to be checked then she went to them.

She was really tired.

Was this another evacuation warning? Leave now before the bridge is cut?

She'd gone to the community meeting. This house was high above the river. Short of a tsunami travelling two hundred miles inland, nothing worse was going to happen than the bridge would give way, the power would go and she'd have to rely on the old kerosene fridge for a few days.

What?

Another knock—and suddenly her irritation turned to fear. She had eight brothers and sisters. A couple of the boys were still young enough to be stupid. Pete… What if…?

What if the car had come with news?

Just open the door and get it over with.

Take a deep breath first.

She tucked her feet into fluffy slippers, wrapped her ancient bathrobe around her favourite pyjamas and padded out to the back porch.

She swung open the door—and Blake Samford was standing in the doorway, holding a baby.

'I think this one's for you,' he said, and handed it over.

She didn't drop it.

To her eternal credit—and thinking back later she was very, very proud of herself—she took the baby, just like the professional she was. Nurse receiving a baby at handover. She gathered the baby as she'd gather any infant she didn't know; any child when she didn't know its history. Taking care to handle it lightly with no pressure, anywhere that might hurt. Cradling it and holding it instinctively against her body, giving warmth as she'd give warmth to any tiny creature.

But for the moment her eyes were on Blake.

He looked almost forbidding. He was looming in her doorway, six feet two or three, wide shoulders, dark, dark eyes made even darker by the faint glow of moonlight, deep black hair, a shadowy figure.

Tall, dark and dangerous.

Heathcliff, she thought, suddenly feeling vaguely hysterical. Very hysterical. Here she was presented with a baby at midnight and she was thinking romance novels?

The dogs were growling behind her. They'd met this guy—he'd been here for three days and she'd seen him outside, talking to them—but he was still a stranger, it was midnight and they didn't know what to make of this bundle in their mistress's arms.

Neither did she, but a baby was more important than the dark, looming stranger on her doorstep.

'What do you mean, you think it's for me?' she managed, trying not to sound incredulous. Trying to sound like he'd just dropped by with a cup of sugar she'd asked to borrow earlier in the day. She didn't want to startle the dogs. She didn't want to startle the baby.

She didn't want to startle herself.

'Someone's obviously made a mistake,' he told her. 'You're the local midwife. I assume they've dumped the baby here to leave it with you.'

'Who dumped it?' She folded back the blanket and looked down into the baby's face. Wide eyes gazed back at her. Gorgeous.

She loved babies. She shouldn't—heaven knew, she'd had enough babies to last her a lifetime— but she had the perfect job now. She could love babies and hand them back.

'I don't know who dumped it,' he said, with exaggerated patience. 'Didn't you hear the car? It came, the baby was dumped, it left.'

She stared up at him, incredulous. He met her gaze, and didn't flinch.

An abandoned baby.

The stuff of fairy-tales. Or nightmares.

She switched her gaze to the little one in her arms.

'Who are you?' she whispered, but of course there was no answer. Instead it wrinkled its small nose, and opened its mouth—and wailed.

Only it wasn't a wail a baby this age should make. It was totally despairing, as if this baby had wailed before and nothing had been forthcoming.

It was a wail that was desperation all by itself—
a wail that went straight to the heart and stayed
there. Maggie had heard hungry babies before, but
none like this. Unbearable. Unimaginable that a
little one could be so needful.

She looked down at the sunken fontanel, the
dry, slightly wrinkled skin. These were classic
signs of dehydration. IV? Fast?

But if the little one could still cry…

It could indeed still cry. It could scream.

'Can you grab the bag from the back of my
car?' she snapped, and whirled and grabbed her
car keys and tossed them to him. 'This little one's
in trouble.'

'Trouble?'

She wheeled away, back to the settee. The fire
was still glowing in the hearth. She could unwrap
the baby without fear of losing warmth. 'Basket,'
she snapped at the dogs, and they headed obe-
diently for their baskets at each side of the fire.
Then, as Blake hesitated, she fixed him with a
look that had made lesser men quail. 'Bag. Now.
Go.'

He headed for the car, feeling a bit…stunned.
And also awed.

The only times he'd seen Maggie Tilden she'd
seemed brisk, efficient and…plain? She dressed
simply for work and she'd been working the whole

time he'd been here. Plain black pants. White blouse with 'Corella Valley Medical Services' emblazoned on the pocket. She wore minimal make-up, and her soft brown curls were tied back in a bouncy ponytail. She was about five feet four or five, she had freckles, brown eyes and a snub nose, and until tonight he would have described her as nondescript.

What he'd just seen wasn't nondescript. It was something far from it.

What?

Cute, he thought, but then he thought no. It was something...deeper.

She'd been wearing faded pink pyjamas, fluffy slippers and an ancient powder-blue bathrobe. Her brown hair, once let loose, showed an auburn burnish. Her curls tumbled about her shoulders and she looked like she'd just woken from sleep. Standing with her dogs by her sides, the fire crackling in the background, she looked...

Adorable?

She looked everything the women in his life weren't. Cosy. Domestic. Welcoming.

And also strong. That glare said he'd better move his butt and get her bag back inside, stat.

She wouldn't know he was a doctor, he thought. When the baby had wailed he'd recognised, as she had, that the little creature was in trouble. The light-bulb over his door had blown long since, but once he'd been under the light of her porch he'd seen the tell-tale signs of dehydration, a baby who looked underweight; malnourished. He'd reached to find a pulse but her movement to defend the child was right. Until she knew what was wrong, the less handling the better.

She was reacting like a midwife at her best, he thought with something of relief. Even if she needed his help right now, this baby wasn't his problem. She was more than capable of taking responsibility.

She was a professional. She could get on with her job and he could move away.

Get the lady her bag. Now.

The bag was a huge case-cum-portable bureau, wedged into the back of an ancient family wagon. He grabbed it and grunted as he pulled it free—it weighed a ton. What was it—medical supplies for the entire valley? How on earth did a diminutive parcel like Maggie handle such a thing?

He was a week out from an appendectomy. He felt internal stitches pull and thought of consequences—and headed for the back door and grabbed the wheelbarrow.

Medical priorities.

If he broke his stitches he'd be no use to anyone. Worse, he'd need help himself.

One bag coming up. By barrow.

* * *

He pushed his way back into the living room and Maggie's eyes widened.

She'd expected landlord with a bag.

What she got was landlord, looking a bit sheepish, with her firewood-carting wheelbarrow, plus bag.

'Appendectomy,' he said before she could say a word. 'Stitches. You don't want two patients.'

Oh, heck. She hadn't thought. He'd told her he was here recovering from an appendectomy. She should have...

'It's fine,' he said, quickly, obviously seeing her remorse. 'As long as you don't mind tyre tracks on your rugs.'

'With my family I'm not used to house-proud. Thanks for getting it. Are you okay?'

'Yes.'

She cast him a sharp, assessing look, and he thought she was working out the truth for herself, and she figured he was telling it.

'If I tell you how, can you make up some formula? This little one's badly dehydrated.'

'Can I see?' he said, over the baby's cries.

The baby was still wailing, desperation personified.

He stooped beside her. He didn't try and touch the baby, just pushed back the coverings further from its face.

Maggie had obviously done a fast check and then rewrapped the infant, leaving the nappy on, tugging open the stained grow suit to the nappy but leaving it on, rewrapping the baby in the same blanket but adding her own, a cashmere throw he'd seen at the end of the sofa.

With the blankets pulled aside and the grow suit unfastened, he could see signs of neglect. This was no rosy, bouncing baby. He could see the tell-tale signs of severe nappy rash, even above the nappy. He could see signs of malnourishment.

She was right about dehydration. They needed to get the little one clean and dry—but first they needed to get fluids in and if it was possible, the best way was by mouth.

'Tell me where, tell me how,' he said, and she shot him a grateful glance and proceeded to do just that. Five minutes later he had a sterilised bottle filled with formula, he offered it to Maggie, she offered it to one tiny baby—who latched on like a leech and proceeded to suck like there was no tomorrow.

The sudden silence was deafening. Even the dogs seemed to sigh in relief.

Maggie's wide, expressive mouth curved into a smile. 'Hey,' she said softly. 'You've just saved yourself from evacuation, hospital and IV drips. Now, let's see what we have here.' She glanced up at Blake. 'Are you man enough to cope with the nappy? I'd normally not try and change a baby in mid-feed but this one's practically walking on its own and I hate to imagine what it's doing to the skin. It needs to be off but I don't want to disturb the baby more than necessary. While the bottle's doing the comforting we might see what we're dealing with.'

He understood. Sort of. There was a medical imperative.

What he'd really like to do was offer to take over the holding and feeding while she coped with the other end, but he'd missed his opportunity. There was no way they should interrupt established feeding when it was so important. This baby needed fluids fast, and Maggie was the one providing them.

So…the other end.

He was a surgeon. He was used to stomach-churning sights.

He'd never actually changed a baby's nappy.

'You'll need a big bowl of warm, soapy water,' she told him. 'The bowl's in the left-hand cupboard by the stove. Get a couple of clean towels from the bathroom and fetch the blue bottle on the top of my bag with the picture of a baby's bottom on the front.'

'Right,' he said faintly, and went to get what he needed, with not nearly the enthusiasm he'd used to make the formula.

Baby changing. He had to learn some time, he supposed. At some stage in the far distant future he and Miriam might have babies. He thought about it as he filled the bucket with skin-temperature water. He and Miriam were professional colleagues having a somewhat tepid relationship on the side. Miriam was dubious about attachment. He was even more dubious.

He suspected what he was facing tonight might make him more so.

'Oi,' Maggie called from the living room. 'Water. Nappy. Stat.'

'Yes, Nurse,' he called back, and went to do her bidding.

CHAPTER TWO

BLAKE removed the nappy and under all that mess… 'She doesn't look like she's been changed for days,' Maggie said, horrified…they found a little girl.

They also found something else. As he tugged her growsuit free from her legs and unwrapped her fully, he drew in a deep breath.

Talipes equinovarus. Club feet. The little girl's feet were pointed inwards, almost at right angles to where they should be.

Severe.

He didn't comment but he felt ill, and it wasn't the contents of the nappy that was doing it. That someone could desert such a child… To neglect her and then just toss her on his doorstep…

How did they know Maggie would be home? Maggie had dogs. How did they know the dogs wouldn't be free to hurt her?

Seeing the extent of the nappy rash, the dehydration—and the dreadful angle of her feet—he had his answer.

Whoever had done this didn't care. This was an imperfect baby, something to be tossed aside, brought to the local midwife, but whether she was home or not didn't matter.

Returning damaged goods, like it or not.

He glanced up at Maggie and saw her face and saw what he was thinking reflected straight back at him. Anger, disgust, horror—and not at the tiny twisted feet. At the moron who'd gunned the car across the bridge, so desperate to dump the baby that he'd take risks. Or *she'd* take risks.

'Surely it was a guy driving that car?' Maggie whispered.

Sexist statement or not? He let it drift as he cleaned the tiny body. The little girl was relaxed now, almost soporific, sucking gently and close to sleep. She wasn't responding to his touch—he could do anything he liked and it was a good opportunity to do a gentle, careful examination.

Maggie was letting him touch now. She was watching as he carefully manipulated the tiny feet, gently testing. As he felt her pulse. As he checked every inch of her and then suggested they lower her into the warm water.

She'd had enough of the bottle on board now to be safe. He doubted she'd respond—as some babies did—to immersion—and it was the easiest and fastest way to get her skin clean.

'You're a medic,' Maggie said, because from the way he was examining her he knew it was obvious. And he knew, instinctively, that this was one smart woman.

'Orthopaedic surgeon.'

She nodded as if he was confirming what she'd suspected. 'Not a lot of babies, then?'

'Um…no.'

'But a lot of feet?'

'I guess,' he agreed, and she smiled at him, an odd little smile that he kind of…liked.

Restful, he thought. She was a restful woman. And then he thought suddenly, strongly, that she was the kind of woman he'd want around in a crisis.

He was very glad she was there.

But the priority wasn't this woman's smile. The priority was one abandoned baby. While Maggie held the bottle—the little girl was still peacefully sucking—he scooped her gently from her arms and lowered her into the warm water.

She hardly reacted, or if she did it was simply to relax even more. This little one had been fighting for survival, he thought. Fighting and losing. Now she was fed and the filth removed. She was in a warm bath in front of Maggie's fire and she was safe. He glanced at Maggie and saw that faint smile again, and he thought that if he was in trouble, he might think of this woman as safety.

If this baby was to be dumped, there was no better place to dump her. Maggie would take care of her. He knew it. This was not a woman who walked away from responsibility.

He glanced around at the dogs on either side of the fire. His father's dogs. When his father had gone into hospital for the last time he'd come down and seen them. They were cattle dogs, Border collies, born and raised on the farm. The last time he'd seen them—six months before his father had died—they'd been scrawny and neglected and he'd thought of the impossibility of taking them back to the city, of giving them any sort of life there.

His father hadn't wanted him here—he'd practically yelled at him to get out. And he'd told him the dogs were none of his business.

Despite the old man's opposition, he'd contacted the local hospital and asked for home visits by a district nurse.

Maggie had taken his father on, and the dogs, and when his father had died she'd suggested she take this place on as well. It had solved two problems—the dogs and an empty farmhouse.

This woman was a problem-solver. She'd solve this little one's problems, too.

The baby had fallen asleep. Maggie removed

the bottle, then took over from him, expertly bathing, carefully checking every inch of the baby's skin, wincing at the extent of the nappy rash, checking arm and leg movement, frowning at a bruise on the baby's shoulder. A bruise at this age… Put down hard? Dropped?

Hit?

'There are basic baby clothes at the bottom of my bag,' she said absently, all her attention on the baby. 'And nappies. Will you fetch them?'

He did, thinking again that no matter who the lowlife was that had cared for the baby until now, at least they'd had the sense to bring her to the right place.

He brought the clothes back as Maggie scooped the baby out of the water, towelled her dry and anointed the sores. Looked again at her feet.

'They should be being realigned now,' he growled, watching as Maggie fingered the tiny toes. 'Three weeks after birth… We're missing the opportunity when the tissue is soft and malleable. The longer we leave it, the longer the treatment period.'

'I've only seen this once before,' Maggie said. 'And not as severe as this.'

'It's severe,' he said. 'But fixable.'

'We have basic X-ray facilities set up at my clinic—at the church hall,' she said tentatively. 'We've brought them in so I can see the difference between greenstick fractures and fractures where I need evacuation.'

'We don't need X-rays tonight. This is long-haul medical treatment.'

'I don't want to call out emergency services unless I have to.' Maggie was still looking worried. 'They have their hands full evacuating people who are being inundated, and in this rain there's no safe place for the chopper to land.'

'There's no urgency.'

'Then we'll worry about tomorrow tomorrow,' she said, her face clearing, and she dressed the little one so gently he thought the dressing was almost a caress in itself. The baby hardly stirred. It was like she'd fought every inch of the way to survive and now she knew she was safe. She knew she was with Maggie.

Maggie wrapped her in her soft cashmere rug—the one she'd tugged from her settee—and handed her over to Blake. He took her without thinking, then sat by the fire with the sleeping baby in his arms as Maggie cleared up the mess.

She was a restful woman, he thought again. Methodical. Calm. How many women would take a child like this and simply sort what was needed? Taking her from peril to safe in an hour?

She was a midwife, he told himself. This was what she did.

This baby was her job.

She was gathering bottles, formula, nappies. Placing them in a basket.

A basket. He'd been drifting off in the warmth but suddenly he was wide awake. What the...?

'Are you thinking we should take her to hospital?' he asked. 'I'm not driving over that bridge.'

'Neither am I,' she said, and brought the basket back to him. 'She looks fine—okay, not fine, neglected, underweight, but nothing so urgent to warrant the risks of crossing the river again. I think she'll be fine with you. I'm just packing what you need.'

'Me?'

'You,' she said, gently but firmly. 'Your baby tonight.'

'I don't want a baby,' he said, stunned.

'You think I do?'

'She was brought to you.'

'No,' she said, still with that same gentleness, a gentleness with a rod of inflexibility straight through the centre. 'She was brought to you. If I didn't think you were capable of caring then I'd step in—of course I would—and I'm here for consulting at any time. But this little one is yours.'

'What are you talking about? You're the midwife.'

'It's got nothing to do about me being a midwife,' she said, and searched the settee until she found what she was looking for. 'I found this when you were making the formula. It was tucked under her blanket.'

It was a note, hastily scribbled on the back of a torn envelope. She handed it to him wordlessly, and then stayed silent as he read.

Dear Big Brother
The old man's dead. He never did anything for me in my life—nothing! You're the legitimate kid, the one that gets everything. You get the farm. You get the kid.
This kid's your father's grandkid. My father's grandkid. I don't want it—just take a look at its feet—they make Sam and me sick. I called it Ruby after my Mum's mum—my grandma—she was the only one ever did anything for me—but that was before I figured how awful the feet were. So it's deformed and we don't want it. Change the name if you like. Get it adopted. Do what you want. Sam and me are heading for Perth so if you need anything signed for adoption or anything stick an ad in the Margaret River paper. If I see it I'll get in touch. Maybe.
Wendy

Silence. A long, long silence.

'Wendy?' Maggie said gently at last.

'My…my half-sister.' He was struggling to take it in. 'Result of one of my father's affairs.'

'Surname?'

'I don't even know that.'

'Whew.' She looked at him, still with that calmness, sympathetic but implacable. 'That's a shock.'

'I… Yes.'

'I think she'll sleep,' Maggie said. 'I suspect she'll sleep for hours. She's not too heavy for you to carry. If you need help, I'm right through the door.'

'This baby isn't mine.' It was said with such vehemence that the little girl—Ruby?—opened her eyes and gazed up at him. And then she closed them again, settling. She was dry, warm and fed. She was in Blake's arms. All was right with her world.

'She's not mine,' Blake repeated, but even he heard the uselessness of his words. Someone had to take responsibility for this baby.

'I'm a nurse, Blake,' Maggie said, inexorably. 'I'm not a parent. Neither are you but you're an uncle. Your sister's left her baby with you. You're family. Let me know if you're in trouble.' She walked across to the porch and opened the door. 'But for now… You have everything you need for the night. I'll pop in in the morning and see how you're going.'

'But I know nothing about babies.'

'You're a doctor,' she said cordially. 'Of course you do.'

'Looking after them?'

'If fifteen-year-old girls can manage it, you can. It's not brain surgery.'

'I'm not a fifteen-year-old.' He was grasping at straws here. 'And I've just had my appendix out.'

'Fifteen-year-olds who've just had Caesareans manage it. How big are babies compared to an appendix? Toughen up.'

He stared at her and she stared right back. She smiled. He thought he sensed sympathy behind her smile, but her smile was still...implacable.

She'd given him his marching orders.

He was holding his niece. *His.*

Maggie was holding the door open; she was still smiling but she was giving him no choice.

With one more despairing glance at this hard-hearted nurse, at the crackling fire, at the sleeping dogs, at a domesticity he hardly recognised, he accepted he had no choice.

He walked out into the night.

With...his baby?

She shouldn't have done it.

The door closed behind him and Maggie stared at it like it was a prosecutor in a criminal court.

Maggie stands accused of abandoning one defenceless baby...

To her uncle. To a doctor. To her landlord.

To a guy recovering from an appendectomy.

To a guy who was capable of driving from Sydney to the valley, to someone who was well on the way to recovery, to someone who was more than capable of looking after his baby.

His baby. Not hers.

This was not her problem. She was a professional. She cared for babies when they needed her medical intervention, and she handed them right back.

She'd done enough of the personal caring to last a lifetime.

She gazed down into the glowing embers of the fire and thought, *My fire.*

It had taken so much courage, so much resolution, so much desperation to find a house of her own. Coreila Valley had practically no rental properties. She had so little money. It had taken all the courage and hope she possessed to gird her loins, approach Blake at the funeral and say, 'I'm looking after your dad's dogs; why don't you let me take care of your house until you put it on the market? I'll live in the housekeeper's residence and I'll keep the place tidy so if you need to use it it'll be ready for you.'

The feeling she'd had when he'd said yes...

Her family still lived less than a mile away, on this side of the river. She was still here for them when they needed her—but she wasn't here for everyone when they needed her. She was not 'good old Maggie' for Blake. This baby was Blake's problem. Blake's niece. Blake's baby, to love or to organise another future for.

If she'd responded to the desperation in his eyes, she'd have a baby here, right now. A baby to twist her heart as it had been twisted all her life.

Eight brothers and sisters. Parents who couldn't give a toss. Maggie, who spent her life having her heart twisted.

'Of course you'll stay home today and look after your brother. Yes, he's ill, but your father and I are heading for Nimbin for a couple of days for the festival... You're a good girl, Maggie.'

Two guitar-toting layabouts with nine kids between them, and Maggie, the oldest, the one who had cared for them all.

She did not need any more responsibility, not in a million years. She had two dogs. She had her own apartment, even if it was only until Blake sold the property.

She was not taking Blake's baby.

And on the other side of the wall, Blake settled the sleeping baby into a cocoon of bedding he'd made in a tugged-out bureau drawer, then stood and stared down at her for a very long time.

Even in two hours she'd changed. Her face had

filled out a little, and the signs of dehydration were fading. She'd been stressed since birth, he thought. She was sleeping as if she was intent on staying asleep, because being awake was frightening and lonely and hard.

He was reading too much into the expression of one sleeping baby. How did he know what she'd been through? How could he possibly guess?

This little one was nothing to do with him. As soon as the river went down he'd hand her over to the appropriate authorities and let them deal with her. But until then...

Maggie should take her, he thought. That was the reasonable plan. A trained midwife, accustomed to dealing with babies every day of her working life, was a far more suitable person to take care of a little one as young as this.

But there was something about Maggie that was implacable. *Not My Problem.* The sign was right up there, hanging over her head like a speech bubble. Said or not, it was what she meant and it was how she'd acted.

She'd sent him home with his niece.

His niece.

He watched her sleep for a while longer. Ruby, he thought.

His niece?

He didn't feel like he had a niece. He didn't feel like he had a sister. He'd only seen his sister that one appalling time, when she'd been little older than Ruby. The moment had been filled with sounds enough to terrify a six-year-old, two women screeching at each other, his father threatening, the baby crying and crying and crying.

He remembered thinking, *Why don't they stop yelling and cuddle her?* He'd even thought of doing it himself, but six was too young to be brave. He'd wanted a cuddle himself. He'd been scared by the yelling and far too young to cope with a baby.

Was he old enough now?

He didn't feel old enough.

He looked down at the tightly wrapped bundle and thought of the tiny feet, facing inwards, needing work to be aligned. He could do that. He was an orthopaedic surgeon. Fixing twisted limbs was what he did.

Not the rest.

Maggie was just through the door. A trained midwife.

The phone rang and he picked it up with relief. It'd be Maggie, he thought, changing her mind, worrying about a baby who should rightly be in her charge.

It wasn't. It was Miriam, doing what she'd promised. 'I'll ring you when I've finished for the day,' she'd told him. 'You don't mind if it's late? You know I'd like to be with you but the board meets next week to appoint the head of ophthalmology and I need to be present to be in the running.'

Of course he'd agreed. They were two ambitious professionals, and a little thing like an appendectomy shouldn't be allowed to get in the way of what was needed for their careers.

A little thing like a baby?

Miriam didn't notice that he was preoccupied. She asked about the floods. He told her briefly that the bridge was blocked, that he was fine, that she needn't worry. Not that she'd have worried anyway. She knew he could take care of himself.

There was little she didn't know about him. They'd been colleagues for years now, in a casual relationship, maybe drifting toward marriage.

And now...

Now he was about to shock her.

'I have a baby,' he told her, and was met with stunned silence. He heard her think it through, regroup, decide he was joking.

'That was fast. You only left town on Friday. You've met a girl, got her pregnant, had a baby...' She chuckled—and then the chuckle died as she heard his continued silence. 'You're not serious?'

He outlined the night's events, the letter, Maggie, their decision not to call for medical evacuation and Maggie's insistence that he do the caring.

He heard her incredulity—and her anger towards a nurse she'd never met.

'She's dumped it on you?'

'I guess.' But it was hardly that.

'Then dump it right back,' she snapped. 'Fast. She has to take care of it. She's the local nurse. It's her job. This is like someone turning up in your office with a fractured leg and you refusing to help.'

'She did help. She bathed and fed her.'

'Her?'

'She's a little girl. Ruby.'

'Don't even think about getting attached.' Miriam's voice was almost a hiss. 'That's what she'll be counting on. You being soft.'

'I'm not soft.'

'I know that, but does she? The nurse? And this sister you've never told me about... Who is she?'

'I know nothing about her other than she's called Wendy. I can't be soft to someone I don't know.'

'So call in the authorities, now. If the bridge is properly cut...'

'It is.'

'How did they get over?'

'They went round the road block and risked their lives.'

'Okay,' she conceded. 'I don't want you risking

your life. You'll probably have to wait till morning but then call for a medical evacuation.'

'She's not sick, Mim.'

'She's not your problem,' Miriam snapped. 'And don't call me Mim. You know I hate it. Call the police, say you have a baby you know nothing about on your doorstep and let them deal with it.'

'This is my father's grandchild. My…niece.'

There was a hiss of indrawn breath. 'So what are you saying? You want to keep it?'

'No!' He was watching the baby while he talked. She'd managed to wriggle a fist free from the bundle Maggie had wrapped her in, and her tiny knuckles were in her mouth. They were giving her comfort, he thought, and wondered how much she'd needed those knuckles in her few short weeks of life.

This was not his problem. Nothing to do with him.

She was his niece. His father's grandchild.

He'd loathed his father. He'd left this place when he'd been six years old and had had two short access visits since. Both had been misery from first to last.

His father had been a bully and a thug.

Maggie had known him better, he thought. Had there been anything under that brutish exterior?

He could ask.

'Just take the baby back to the midwife and insist,' Miriam was saying. 'It's her professional responsibility. You could...I don't know...threaten to have her struck off if she doesn't?'

'For handing a baby back to her family?'

'You're not her family.'

'I'm all she has.'

'Her parents are all she has. The police can find them tomorrow. Meanwhile, lean on the nurse. You're recovering, Blake. You do not need this hassle. Okay, misconduct mightn't fly but there are other ways. You're her landlord. Threaten to evict her.'

'Mim—'

'Just do whatever you need to do,' she snapped. 'Look, love, I rang to tell you about the paper I presented this afternoon. It went really well. Can I finally tell you about it?'

'Of course,' he said, and he thought that would settle him. He could stand here and listen to Miriam talk medicine and he could forget all about his little stranger who'd be gone tomorrow.

And he could also forget about the woman who'd refused to take her.

Maggie.

Why was he thinking about Maggie?

He was remembering her at the funeral. It had been pouring. She'd been dressed in a vast overcoat and gumboots, sensible garments in the tiny, country graveyard. She'd stomped across to him, half-hidden by her enormous umbrella, and she'd put it over him, enclosing him for the first time, giving him his only sense of inclusion in this bleak little ceremony.

'I took on your father's dogs because I couldn't bear them to be put down,' she'd said. 'But I'm sharing a too-small house with my too-big family. The dogs make the situation unworkable. I assume your dad's farm will be empty for a while. It has a housekeeper's residence at the back. If I pay a reasonable rent, how about you let me live there until you decide what to do with it?'

'Yes,' he'd said without any hesitation, and he'd watched something akin to joy flash across her face.

'Really?'

'Really.'

'You won't regret it,' she'd said gruffly. 'The dogs and I will love it.' Then she'd hesitated and looked across at the men filling in the open grave. 'He was a hard man, your father,' she'd said softly. 'I'm sorry.'

And he'd thought, uncomfortably, that she understood.

Did this whole district understand? That he and his father had had no relationship at all?

They weren't a family.

Family...

His mother had gone on to three or four more

relationships, all disastrous. He'd never worked out the concept of family. Now…

He listened on to Miriam and he watched the sleeping baby. Would he and Miriam ever have babies? Family?

Now wasn't the time to ask, he thought, and he grimaced as he realised he hadn't heard a word she'd said for the last few minutes.

Focus, he told himself. Do what the lady says. Concentrate on medicine and not baby. Tomorrow give the baby back to Maggie or get rid of it some other way. Do whatever it takes. This was an aberration from the past.

One baby, with twisted feet and no one to care for her. An aberration?

He carried on listening to Miriam and he thought, Maggie's just through the wall. She might even be listening to half this conversation.

The thought was unnerving.

Forget it, he thought. Forget Maggie. And the baby?

Do whatever it takes.

If only she wasn't sucking her knuckles. If only she wasn't twisting his heart in a way that made him realise a pain he'd felt when he'd been six years old had never been resolved.

She was his father's grandchild. She was the child of his half-sister.

Family?

It was his health that was making him think like this, he told himself. He'd had his appendix out barely a week before, and it had been messy. He was tired and weaker than he cared to admit, and he was staying in a house that held nothing but bad memories.

He had a sudden, overwhelming urge to thump a hole in the wall in the sitting room. Let his father's dogs through.

See Maggie.

Heaven knew what Miriam was saying. He'd given up trying to listen. It had been an important paper she'd presented. Normally he'd listen and be impressed. Tonight, though, he looked at one tiny baby, sleeping cocooned in Maggie's cashmere blanket, and suddenly he felt tired and weak—and faintly jealous of the deep sleep, the total oblivion.

And he also felt…alone.

If the bridge was safe, maybe he'd suggest Miriam come down.

Don't be nuts, he told himself. She'd never come, and even if she did there'd be nothing for her to do.

She wouldn't care for a baby.

He had to.

Baby. Floods. Maggie. The images were drifting around his head in a swirl of exhausted confusion.

Baby. Floods. Maggie.

'I need to go,' he told Miriam, cutting her off in mid-sentence. 'Sorry, love, but I'll ring you back tomorrow. The baby needs me.'

'The midwife—'

'She's gone to sleep,' he said. 'That's where I'm heading, too. Hours and hours of sleep. I just have to get one baby called Ruby to agree.'

CHAPTER THREE

MAGGIE fed the hens at six the next morning and she heard Ruby crying.

She sorted feed, cut and chopped a bit of green stuff and threw it into the chookpen—there'd been a fox sniffing around and she wasn't game to let them out. She collected the eggs.

Ruby was still crying.

It wasn't her business, she told herself. Not yet. What district nurse dropped in at this hour? She'd make a professional visit a little later. Meanwhile, she should make breakfast and head to the makeshift clinic she'd set up in the back of the local hall, to do last-minute preparations and sort equipment.

That could wait, though, she conceded. The authorities had only put the roadblock up yesterday. Everyone who'd needed anything medical had had two days' warning. The weather forecast had been implacable. The water's coming. Get your stock to high ground. Evacuate or get in any supplies you need because it may be a week or more before the river goes down.

The pharmacy over the river and the doctors at the Valley Hospital had worked tirelessly over the last few days, checking every small complaint, filling prescriptions to last a month. The Valley people had seen floods before. There'd be no last-minute panic.

There would, however, be no doctor on this side of the river for a while.

Except Blake. The thought was strangely comforting.

Floods often meant trauma as people did stupid things trying to save stock, trying to fix roof leaks, heaving sandbags. Knowing she had a doctor on this side of the river, even one recovering from an appendectomy, was a blessing. If he'd help.

And if she expected him to help…maybe she could help him with his baby?

She'd made it clear she wasn't taking responsibility. That was what he wanted her to do, but even if she agreed, she couldn't care for a newborn as well as for the medical needs of everyone on this side of the river.

So she'd been firm, which wasn't actually like her. But firmness was her new resolve.

Right now, though, she was figuring that firm didn't mean cruel. The guy really didn't know anything about babies. If she had a teenage mum floundering, she'd move in to help.

Hold that thought, she decided, and she almost grinned at the thought of one hunky Blake Samford in the role of teen mum.

She'd help—even at six a.m.

So she knocked on his back door and waited. No answer. The wailing got louder.

She pushed the door tentatively inwards and went to investigate.

Blake was standing in the living room, in front of the vast, stone fireplace that was the centre of this huge, old homestead. The room was as it always was when she did her weekly check on the whole house, huge and faded and comfortable. A vast Persian rug lay on the worn, timber floor. The room was furnished with squishy leather settees, faded cushions and once opulent drapes, now badly in need of repair. The fire in the vast fireplace made it warm and homelike. The house was a grand old lady, past her prime but still graciously decorous.

Not so the guy in front of the fire. He was wearing boxer shorts and nothing else. He looked big, tanned, ripped—and not decorous at all.

Maggie was a nurse. She was used to seeing human bodies in all shapes and sizes.

She wasn't used to seeing this one.

Tall, dark and dangerous. Where had that phrase

come from? She wasn't sure, but she knew where it was now. It was flashing in her head. Danger, danger, danger. A girl should turn round and walk right out of there.

Except he was holding a baby—all the wrong way—and his look spoke of desperation.

She put down her bucket of eggs, headed wordlessly to the kitchen to wash her hands, then came back and took the little one into her arms.

Blake practically sagged with relief.

'You need to wrap her,' she said, brisk and efficient because brisk and efficient seemed the way to go. 'She's exhausted.'

She cradled the little one tightly against her and felt an almost imperceptible relaxation. Babies seemed to respond instinctively to those who knew the ropes. To their mothers, who learned from birth how to handle them. To midwives, who'd delivered too many babies to count.

'She's been safely in utero for nine months,' she told him. 'She's been totally confined, and now her legs and arms are all over the place. It feels weird and frightening. She can handle it if she's relaxed, but not if she's tired and hungry.'

'But she won't feed,' he said helplessly, motioning to the bottle on the table. 'I can't—'

'She's gone past it. She needs to be settled first.' She sat on the settee and almost disappeared. These settees must be older than Blake, she thought. Old and faded and stuffed loosely with goosedown. She'd never seen such huge settees.

In truth she was finding it hard to thinking about settees. Not with that body…

Get a grip. Settees. Baby.

Not Blake.

She set about rewrapping Ruby, bundling her tightly so those flailing little legs and arms could relax, and the baby attached to them would feel secure. But she was a midwife. Bundling babies was second nature. She had more than enough time to think about settees and baby—and Blake Samford's body.

Which was truly awesome. Which was enough to make a girl…make a girl…

Think unwisely. Think stupid, in fact. This was her landlord—a guy who wanted to get rid of a baby.

You show one hint of weakness and you'll have a baby on your hands, she told herself. And if you fall for this baby…

She'd fallen for two dogs. That was more than enough.

She lived in this man's house as a tenant, and that was all. If babies came with the territory then she moved out.

This was dumb. She was thinking dramatic when the situation simply needed practical. This guy had a problem and she could help him, the same way she'd help any new parent. She'd help and then she'd leave.

Ruby was still wailing, not with the desperation of a moment ago but with an I-want-something-and-I-want-it-now wail.

She lifted the bottle and flicked a little milk on her wrist. Perfect temperature. She offered it, one little mouth opened and accepted—and suddenly the noise stopped.

The silence was magical.

She smiled. Despite very real qualms in this case, Maggie Tilden did love babies. They sucked you in.

Her mother had used that to her advantage. Maggie's mother loved having babies, she just didn't like caring for them.

Over to Maggie.

And that was what Blake wanted. Over to Maggie.

Do not get sucked in, she told herself desperately. Do not become emotionally involved.

Anything but that. Even looking at Blake.

At his chest. At the angry red line she could see emerging from the top of his shorts.

Appendix. Stitches. Even if the external ones had been removed, it'd take weeks for the internal ones to dissolve.

'So no keyhole surgery for you?' she asked,

trying to make her voice casual, like this was a normal neighbourly chat. 'You didn't choose the right surgeon?'

'I chose the wrong appendix,' he said, glancing down at his bare abs. 'Sorry. I'll cover up.'

'I'm not squeamish about an appendix scar,' she told him. 'I'm a nurse. So things were messy, huh?

'Yes.'

'No peritonitis?'

'I'm on decent antibiotics.'

Her frown deepened. 'Are you sure you're okay to stay on this side of the river?'

'Of course.'

But she was looking at problems she hadn't foreseen. Problems she hadn't thought about. 'If there's the least chance of infection... I assumed you'd had keyhole surgery. If I'd known...'

'You would have ordered me to leave?'

'I'd have advised you to leave.'

'You're in charge?'

'That's just the problem,' she said ruefully. 'I am. Until the water goes down there's no way I can get anyone to medical help. There's just me.'

'And me.'

She nodded, grateful that he was acknowledging he could help in a crisis—having a doctor on this side was wonderful but one who'd so recently had surgery? 'That's fine,' she told him. 'Unless you're the patient.'

'I don't intend to be the patient.' He was look-ing down at the blissfully sucking baby with be-musement. 'Why couldn't I do that?'

'You could. You can.' She rose and handed the bundle over, bottle and all, and Blake was left standing with an armload of baby. 'Sit,' she told him. 'Settle. Bond.'

'Bond?'

'You're her uncle. I suspect this little one needs all the family she can get.'

'It's she who needs medical help,' he said, al-most savagely, and Ruby startled in his arms.

'Sit,' Maggie said again. 'Settle.'

He sat. He settled, as far as a man with an arm-load of baby could settle.

He looked…stunning, Maggie thought. Bare chested, wearing only boxer shorts, his dark hair raked and rumpled, his five o'clock shadow a few hours past five o'clock. Yep, stunning was the word for it.

It'd be wise if she failed to be stunned. She needed to remember she was here for a postnatal visit. Maternal health nurse visiting brand-new parent…

Who happened to be her landlord.

Who happened to be a surgeon—who was tell-ing her the baby had medical needs.

She needed to pay attention to something other

than how sexy he looked, one big man, almost naked, cradling a tiny baby.

With medical needs. Get serious.

'If you think her legs are bad enough to require immediate medical intervention I can organise helicopter evacuation,' she said. She knelt and unwrapped the blanket from around the tiny feet and winced.

'I can't believe her mother rejected her because of her feet,' she whispered, and Blake shook his head.

'No mother rejects her baby because of crooked feet.'

'Some fathers might. Some do. A daughter and an imperfect one at that. If the mother's weak…'

'Or if the mother's on drugs…'

'There doesn't seem any sign of withdrawal,' Maggie said, touching the tiny cheek, feeling the way the baby's face was filling out already. 'If her mother's a drug addict, this little one will be suffering withdrawal herself.'

'She's three weeks old,' Blake said. 'She may well be over it. But if she was addicted, those first couple of weeks will have been hell. That and the talipes may well have been enough for her to be rejected.'

'That and the knowledge that you've come home,' Maggie said thoughtfully. 'If your sister knows you're here, and thinks you're in a position to care for her, then she might see you as a way out.'

'She's not my sister.'

'Your father is her father.'

'I don't even know her surname.'

'No, but I do,' she said smoothly. 'She's Wendy Runtland, twenty-nine years old, and she lives on a farmlet six miles on the far side of the base hospital. Ruby was born on the twenty-first of last month. Wendy only stayed overnight and refused further assistance. The staff were worried. They'd organised a paediatrician to see the baby to assess her feet but Wendy discharged herself—and Ruby—before he got there.'

'How the—?'

'I'm a midwife employed by the Valley Health Service,' she told him. 'If I'm worried about babies, I can access files. I rang the hospital last night and asked for a search for a local baby born with talipes. Ruby's the only fit. The file's scanty. No antenatal care. First baby. Fast, hard labour with a partner present for some of the time. They were both visibly upset by the baby's feet and there's a note in the file that the guy was angry and abusive.

'The next morning Wendy discharged herself and the baby against medical advice. There were no grounds to involve the police but staff did notify Social Services. The maternal health nurse has tried to make home visits but each time she's found gates locked and dogs that didn't allow her to go further. There's a phone number but the phone's been slammed down each time she's rung. You might have more luck. You want to try while I check the bridge?'

'What's to check?'

He looked almost dumbfounded, she thought. Man left with abandoned baby. Surgeon way out of his comfort zone.

'I've been listening to the radio and it's still raining up north,' she said evenly. 'There's a vast mass of water coming down. If the water keeps rising it might be a while before you can get her to Social Services.'

'Social Services?'

'Unless we can get her back to her mother— or unless you want her—I assume that's where she'll be placed. Either way, the decision has to be made soon. Those feet need attention now, although I assume you know that.'

'I know it,' he growled, and then he fell silent.

He stared down at the baby in his arms and she thought...there was something there, some link.

Family.

He'd said he didn't have a sister. He'd said he didn't even know her full name.

This was a guy who was an intelligent, skilled surgeon, she thought, a guy who'd know how to keep his emotions under control. But his recent surgery would have weakened him, and a sleepless night would have weakened him still more.

She had a feeling this guy didn't let his defences down often, but they were down now. He was gazing at the child in his arms and his face said he didn't know where to go with this.

Evacuate her? Hand her over to Social Welfare? Keep her until the river went down?

Risk attachment?

She couldn't help him. It was his decision.

'I'll try and phone Wendy,' he said at last, and she nodded and got to her feet and collected her eggs.

'Excellent. I'll leave some of these in your kitchen. Tell me how you go.'

'Maggie?'

She paused. Met his gaze. Saw desperation.

'Stay here while I ring,' he said, and she thought maybe she could at least do that.

But as he handed back the now fed, sleeping Ruby, and she gathered her into her arms and watched Blake head for the phone, she thought… she thought…

She thought this was as far as she should go.

Babies did things to her. Her mother had used that, played on it, trapped her with it. And now…

The sight of Blake was doing things to her as well. He was all male, one gorgeous hunk of testosterone, but it wasn't that that was messing with her head.

It was the way he'd looked at Ruby—and the way he'd looked at her when he'd asked her to stay.

Under that strength was pure vulnerability.

Maggie had lived most of her life in this valley and she'd heard stories about this family; this man. His mother had been glamorous and aloof and cold, and she'd walked out—justifiably—when Blake had been six. His father had been a womanising brute.

Blake may come from the richest family in the district but the locals had felt sorry for him when he'd been six, and that sympathy hadn't been lessened by anything anyone had heard since.

What sort of man was he now? Like his mother? Like his father?

She couldn't tell. She was seeing him at his most vulnerable. He was wounded, shocked, tired and burdened by a baby he didn't know.

Don't judge now, she told herself. Don't get any more involved than you already are.

Except…she could stay while he rang his sister.

She sank down on the settee and put her feet towards the fire. This was a great room. A family room.

She lived on the other side of the wall. Remember it, she told herself.

Meanwhile, she cuddled one sleeping baby and she listened.

Blake had switched to speakerphone. He wanted to share.

She could share, she decided, at least this much.

Blake punched in the numbers Maggie had given him and a woman answered on the second ring. Sounding defensive. Sounding like she'd expected the call.

'Wendy?'

There was a long silence and Maggie wondered if she'd slam down the receiver as she'd slammed it down on the district nurse.

'Blake,' she said at last. She sounded exhausted. Drained. Defeated.

The baby was three weeks old, Maggie thought, and wondered about postnatal depression.

'You know my name,' Blake was saying, tentatively, feeling his way. 'I didn't even know yours.'

'That would be because our father acknowledged you.'

'I'm sorry.'

'Bit late to be sorry now,' she hissed. 'Thirty years.'

'Wendy, what my father did or didn't do to you isn't anything to do with me.'

'You got the farm.'

'We can talk about that,' he said evenly. 'But right now we need to talk about your daughter.'

'She's not my daughter,' she snapped.'I didn't even want her in the first place. Now Sam says he won't even look at her.'

'Too right, I won't,' a man's voice growled, and Maggie realised it wasn't only Blake who was on speakerphone. 'We never wanted kids, neither of us. We're going to Western Australia, but there's no way we're taking a deformed rat with us. By the time Wendy realised she was pregnant it was too late to get rid of it but neither of us want it. We should have left it at the hospital, but all them forms… Anyway, she's getting her tubes tied the minute we get settled, and that's it. If you want the kid adopted, we'll sign the papers, but we don't have time for any of that now. Meanwhile, the kid's yours. Do what you like with it. We're leaving.'

'Let me talk to Wendy,' again, he said. 'Wendy?'

Wendy came on the line again, just as defensive. 'Yeah?'

'Is this really what you want?' he asked urgently. 'This shouldn't be about our past. It's now. It's Ruby. Do you really want to abandon your daughter?'

'Yeah,' Wendy said, and defence gave way to bitterness. 'Yeah, I do, but I'm not abandoning her. I'm giving her to you. My family's done nothing for me, ever, so now it's time. I don't want this kid, so you deal with it, big brother. Your problem.'

And the phone was slammed down with a force that must have just about cracked the receiver at the other end.

Silence.

Deathly silence.

Blake put the phone back in its charger like it might shatter. Like the air around him might shatter.

Maggie looked at his face and looked away.

She looked down at the little girl in her arms.

Deformed rat.

Thank God she was only three weeks old. Thank God she couldn't understand.

Suddenly the way her mother had looked at Maggie's brothers and sisters flooded back to her. Over and over she remembered her mother, exhausted from childbirth, arriving home from hospital, sinking onto her mound of pillows in the bed that was her centre, handing over the newest arrival to her eldest daughter.

'You look after it, Maggie.'

Her mother wasn't close to as bad as this, but there were similarities. Her parents did what they had to do, but no more. Life was fun and frivolous, and responsibility was something to be handed over to whoever was closest.

Her mother liked being pregnant. Her parents liked the weird prestige of having a big family, but they wanted none of the responsibility that went with it.

Deformed rat.

She found herself hugging the little one closer, as if she could protect her from the words. From the label.

Abandoned baby.

Deformed rat.

And then the baby was lifted from her arms. Blake had her, was cradling her, holding her as a man might hold his own newborn. The way he held her was pure protection. It was anger and frustration and grief. It was an acknowledgement that his world had changed.

'She won't change her mind,' he said grimly, and it was hardly a question.

'I suspect not,' Maggie whispered. 'Not after three weeks. Mothers often reject straight after birth if there's something seriously wrong—or if depression or psychosis kicks in—but she's cared for her—after a fashion—for three weeks now. And the anger... I'm thinking this is a thought-out decision, as much as either of them sound like they can think anything out. After three weeks with this one, there should be an unbreakable bond. If there's not, it won't form now. All we can hope for is to maintain contact.'

'You'd want Ruby to maintain contact with a family who think of her as…?' He broke off, sounding appalled. 'We'll have to organise adoption. Surely there's a family who'll want her.'

'There will be,' Maggie said. 'Of course. But without the papers…she'll need to go into foster-care first.'

'And let me guess, there's no foster-carers over this side of the river.'

'I'm organising evacuation,' she said, and he stared at her. As well he might. This decision had been made a whole two seconds ago.

'Sorry?'

'For both of you,' she said briskly. 'I read up on talipes last night. I haven't seen a baby with it before but I know what needs to be done. She needs careful manipulation and casts, starting now. The Ponseti technique talks about long casts on both legs, changed weekly. I can't do that. Then there's the fact that you had appendicitis with complications a week ago.'

'I didn't have complications.'

'So why didn't you have keyhole surgery?' She fixed him with a look she'd used often on recalcitrant patients. 'Right. Complications. So in summary, I have a man who may end up needing urgent help from previous surgery. I have a baby

who needs urgent medical attention. The rain has
eased this morning but the forecast is that more
storms will hit tonight. I can get you out of here
right now. You can have Ruby back in Sydney in
the best of medical care, organising foster-care,
organising anything you need, by this afternoon.
I'll make the call now.'

'You're kicking me out?'

'You have medical training, too,' she said. 'You
know it's for the best.'

She was right.

Of course she was right. If she made the call, all
problems would be solved. Evacuation was justified. If he didn't accept the offer—the order?—
he could well end up stuck here with a baby for
a couple of weeks.

He could take Ruby back to Sydney, right now.

He could be home in his own, clean, clinical
apartment tonight, with Ruby handed over to car-
ers, and all this behind him.

Maggie was waiting. She stood calmly, her
bucket of eggs in her hand, ready to take action.

He thought, stupidly, Who'll eat the eggs if I
go?

It was sensible to go.

The phone rang again. He picked it up without
thinking. It was still on speakerphone—his father's landline. He half expected it to be Wendy,
but it was a child's voice, shrill and urgent.

'Maggie?'

The eggs were back on the floor so fast some must have broken, and Maggie had the phone in an instant.

'Susie, what's wrong?'

'Christopher's bleeding…' On the other end of the line, the child hiccupped on a sob and choked.

'No crying, Susie,' Maggie said, and it was a curt order that had Blake's eyes widen. It sounded like sergeant major stuff. 'You know it doesn't help. What's happened?'

'He slid on the wet roof and he cut himself,' Susie whimpered. 'His blood is oozing out from the top of his leg, and Mum's screaming and Pete said to ring and say come.'

'I'm coming,' Maggie said, still in the sergeant major voice. 'But first you listen, Susie, and listen hard. Get a sheet out of the linen cupboard and roll it up so it's a tight, tight ball. Then you go out to Christopher, you tell Mum to shut up and keep away—can you do that, Susie? Imagine you're me and just do it—and tell Pete to put the ball of sheet on his leg and press as hard as he's ever pressed in his life. Tell him to sit on it if he must. He has to stop the bleeding. Can you do that, love?'

'I… Yes.'

'I'll be there before Mum even stops yelling,' Maggie said. 'You just make Pete keep pressing, and tell everyone I'm on my way.'

CHAPTER FOUR

ONE minute she was readying Blake for medical evacuation. The next she was heading a mile down the road to the ramshackle farmhouse where her parents and four of their nine children lived.

With Blake and baby.

How had it happened?

She hardly had time to wonder. Her entire concentration was on the road—apart from a little bit that was aware of the man beside her.

She'd headed for the door, out to the wagon, but by the time she'd reversed and turned, Blake had been in pants and shirt, standing in front of the car, carrying Ruby.

'If he's bleeding out, you'll need me,' he'd snapped, and she hadn't argued. She'd fastened a seemingly bemused Ruby into the baby carrier she always carried—as district nurse her car was always equipped for carting kids—and now she was heading home and Blake was hauling his shoes on while she drove.

Christopher was twelve years old. He'd had more accidents than she could remember.

'I should never have left them,' she muttered, out loud but addressed to herself.

'You should never have left home?' Blake had tied his shoes and was now buttoning his shirt. He was almost respectable. Behind them, Ruby had settled into the baby carrier, like this was totally satisfactory—baby being taken for an after-breakfast drive by Mum and Dad.

Mum and Dad? Ha!

'My parents aren't responsible people,' Maggie said through gritted teeth. 'They should have been neutered at birth.'

'Um…there's a big statement.' Blake looked thoughtful. 'That'd mean there'd have been no Maggie.'

'And none of the other eight they won't look after,' she snapped. 'But Nickie, Louise, Raymond and Donny are out of the valley now, studying. Susie's ten—she's the youngest. I thought they were getting independent. With me only a mile away I thought they'd be safe.'

'They're as safe as if you were living there and gone to the shops for milk,' Blake said, and she let the thought drift—and the tight knot of fear and guilt unravelled a bit so that only fear remained.

And the fear was less because this man was sitting beside her.

But she still didn't know what she was dealing with. If Chris had cut his femoral artery...

'She said oozing,' Blake said, as if his thoughts were running concurrent with hers. 'If it was the artery she'd have used a more dramatic word.'

The fear backed off a little, too. She allowed a glimmer of hope to enter the equation, but she didn't ease her foot from the accelerator.

'No hairpin bends between here and your place?' Blake asked, seemingly mildly.

'No.'

'Good,' Blake said. 'Excellent. No aspersions on your driving, but Ruby and I are very pleased to hear it.'

They pulled up outside a place that looked like a cross between a house and a junkyard. The house looked almost derelict, a ramshackle, weather-board cottage with two or three shonky additions tacked onto the back. The veranda at the front was sagging, kids' toys and bikes were everywhere and Blake could count at least five car bodies—or bits of car bodies. An old white pony was loosely tethered to the veranda, and a skinny, teenage girl came flying down from the veranda to meet them.

'Maggie, round the back, quick...'

Maggie was out of the car almost before it had stopped, and gone.

Blake was left with the girl.

Maggie had left her bag. The girl was about to dart off, too, but Blake grabbed her by the shoulder and held on.

'I'm a friend of Maggie's,' he said curtly. 'I'm a doctor. Will you stay with the baby? Take care of her while I help Maggie?'

The girl stared at him—and then stared into the car at the baby.

'Yes,' she whispered. 'Blood makes me wobble.'

As long as babies didn't, Blake thought, but it was cool and overcast, Ruby was asleep and in no danger of overheating, and Maggie might well need him more.

He thrust the girl into the passenger seat and she sat as if relieved to be there. Then he hauled open Maggie's bag. Maggie was methodical, he thought. Equipment was where he expected it to be. He couldn't handle the whole bag but he grabbed worst-case scenario stuff and headed behind the house at a run.

His stitches pulled, but for the first time since the operation, he hardly noticed.

Behind the house was drama. Maggie was already there, stooped over a prostrate child. Around them was a cluster of kids of assorted ages, and a woman was down on her knees, wailing. 'Maggie, it's making me sick. Maggie...'

The kids were ignoring the woman. They were totally intent on Maggie—who was totally intent on the child she was caring for.

Christopher was a miniature version of Maggie, he thought as he knelt beside her to see what they were dealing with. Same chestnut hair. Same freckles.

No colour at all.

Maggie was making a pad out of a pile of sheets lying beside her. An older boy—Peter?—his face as white as death—was pressing hard on a bloodied pad on his brother's thigh. As Blake knelt beside her, Maggie put her own pad in position.

'Okay, Pete, lift.'

The boy lifted the pad away, and in the moment before Maggie applied her tighter pad, Blake saw a gash, eight to ten inches long. Pumping. Not the major artery—he'd be dead by now if he'd hit that, but bad enough.

Leg higher than heart.

Maggie had replaced the pad and was pressing down again. Blood was oozing out the sides.

Whoever had grabbed the sheets had grabbed what looked like the contents of the linen cupboard. He grabbed the whole pile and wedged them under the boy's thighs, elevating the leg.

Maggie moved with him and they moved effort-lessly into medical-team mode.

The oozing blood was slowing under her hands, but not enough. Pressure could only do so much.

Maggie was looking desperate. She knew what was happening.

Blake was already checking and rechecking the equipment in his hands. Hoping to hell her sterilisation procedures were thorough. Knowing he had no choice.

He'd wrapped the stuff in a sterile sheet he'd pulled from plastic. He laid it on the grass, set it out as he'd need it, then hauled on sterile gloves.

'On the count of three, take your hands away,' he said to Maggie, and she glanced up at him, terror everywhere, saw his face, steadied, and somehow moved more solidly into medical mode.

'You're assisting, Nurse,' he said flatly, calmly. 'Don't let me down. Pete, hold your brother's shoulders, tight. Christopher, I'm about to stop the bleeding. It'll hurt but only for a moment. Grit your teeth and bear it.'

He'd swabbed and slid in pain relief while he talked but he didn't have time for it to take effect.

'Ready?' he snapped to his makeshift theatre team.

'R-ready,' Maggie faltered.

'You stay calm on me,' he snapped. 'Pete, have you got those shoulders? Not one movement. Use all your strength to hold your brother still. Chris, are you ready to bite the bullet, like they say in the movies? We need you to be a hero.'

'I… Yes.'

'Good kid,' Blake said. 'You don't need to pretend—you are a hero. I need to hurt you to stop the bleeding but I'll be fast. This is superhero country. Pretend you're armed with kryptonite and hold on.'

Maggie was terrified.

She was a nurse assisting a surgeon in Theatre, and somehow the second took priority over the first. Blake's calm authority, his snapped, incisive instructions, the movements of his fingers…it was all that mattered. It had to be all that mattered.

Instead of being a terrified sister, she was a theatre assistant and only that. She was focussed entirely on anticipating Blake's needs, swabbing away blood so she could see what he was doing, handing him what he needed as he needed it.

A torn artery…

Worse, it had retracted into the wound. She could see the blood seeping from the top of the rip in the skin. This was no exposed artery to be simply tied off.

If there was time for anaesthetic…

There wasn't, and she held her breath as Blake

produced a scalpel and fast, neatly, precisely, extended the tear just enough…just enough…

Chris jerked and cried out, but magically Pete held him still.

She swabbed and could see.

He was before her. The scalpel was back in her hand—not dropped when they might need it again—and forceps taken instead. Somehow she'd had them ready.

Blake was working inside the wound, manoeuvring, while she tried desperately to keep the wound clear, let him see what he was dealing with.

'Got it,' he said, amazingly calmly, as if the issue had never been in doubt, and almost as he said it, the bleeding slowed.

He was using the forceps to clamp.

'Suture,' he said.

She prepared sutures faster than she'd thought possible. She watched as his skilled fingers moved in and out, in and out.

She swabbed and cut and cleaned and she thought, Thank you, God.

Thank you, Blake.

He'd done it. The bleeding had slowed to almost nothing. He sat back and felt the same sense of overwhelming dizziness he always felt after such drama.

Cope first, faint second? It was an old edict instilled in him by a long-ago surgery professor when he'd caught his knees buckling.

'There's no shame in a good faint,' the professor had said. 'We all suffer from reaction. Just learn to delay it.'

He'd delayed it—and so had Maggie. In no other circumstances would he have permitted a relative to assist in a procedure on a family member. For her to hold it together...

She'd done more than that. She'd been calm, thorough, brilliant.

They weren't out of the woods yet. What was needed now was replacement volume. He felt Chris's pulse and flinched. With this blood pressure he was at risk of cardiac arrest.

They needed fluids, now.

But Maggie's capacious bag had provided all he needed. Thank God for Maggie's bag. Thank God for district nurses.

While Maggie worked under orders, applying a rough dressing that kept the pressure up—he'd need to remove it later when the pain relief kicked in fully to do a neater job—he lifted the boy's arm, swabbed it fast and slid in the IV. A moment later he taped it safely, grabbed a bag of saline and started it running.

He checked the pulse and checked again that he had adrenalin close.

He checked the pulse again and decided not yet.

'Do we have plasma?' he asked.

'At the clinic,' Maggie said. 'Ten minutes' drive away.'

It wasn't worth risking driving for yet. He'd run the saline and wait.

The lad seemed close to unconscious, dazed, hazy, hardly responding, but as the saline dripped in and the drugs took effect, they saw a tiny amount of colour return.

The pulse under Blake's fingers regained some strength.

Around them the family watched, horrified to stillness, willing a happy ending. As did Blake. As, he thought, did Maggie. Her face was almost as white as the child's.

This child was her brother.

Brothers and sisters.

He thought suddenly of the baby he'd seen thirty years before when he'd been six years old. His sister. He'd never had this connection, he thought, and then he thought of Ruby and wondered if this was a second chance.

It was a crazy time to think of one tiny baby.

Think of Christopher.

The saline dripped in. He kept his fingers on the little boy's pulse, willing the pressure to rise, and finally it did. Christopher seemed to stir from semi-consciousness and he whimpered.

'Christopher, love, keep still,' Maggie said urgently, but he heard the beginnings of relief in her voice. 'It's okay. You've cut your leg badly, so you need to keep it still, but Dr Samford's fixed it. It'll be fine. What a duffer you were to try and climb on the wet roof.'

'You slide faster when it's wet,' he whispered. 'But it hurts. I won't do it again.'

Blake let out his breath. He hadn't actually been aware that he hadn't been breathing but now...

He remembered another rule instilled into him a long time ago by the professor who'd taken him for his paediatric term. 'Rule of thumb for quick triage. If a child is screaming, put it at the end of the queue. If it's quiet but whinging, middle. If it's silent, front, urgent, *now.*'

Christopher had suddenly moved from front of the line to the middle.

He glanced at Maggie and she seemed to sag. There was relief but also weariness. Desperation.

He glanced around and he thought, How many times had this scene played out? Maggie, totally responsible.

The mother—a crazy, hippy-dressed mass of sodden hysteria, was incoherent in the background, slumped on the grass crying, holding onto yet another kid, a little girl who looked about ten. As Blake watched, the little girl tried to pull away to come across to Maggie, but her mother held her harder.

'Hold me, Susie,' she whimpered. 'I'll faint if you don't. Oh, my God, you kids will be the death of me.'

Let her faint, he thought grimly, and glanced again at Maggie and saw a look...

Like a deer trapped in headlights.

How much responsibility did this woman carry for this family?

'Swap places and I'll bind it,' he told her. He needed to take the pressure off Maggie so she could react to the needs of these kids—to Chris but also to brave Pete, who'd held his brother all this time, and to Susie, who'd held her mother. 'Do we have somewhere we can stitch it properly?' He glanced at the house—and Maggie's mother—and thought, I just bet it's not clean inside.

'Maggie's not stitching me,' Christopher whimpered. 'She hurts.'

'You've stitched your brother before?' he demanded, astounded.

Maggie gave a rueful smile. 'Not unless I've have no choice,' she told him. 'But Christopher doesn't give his family many choices.'

'You have a choice now,' he said, still seeing that trapped look. 'I can do this. You said you've set up a clinic. With a surgery?'

'A small one.'

'Excellent.' He smiled down at Christopher. 'If you'll accept me as a substitute for your sister, we'll bind your leg so you don't make a mess of her car, then we'll take you to the clinic she's set up. I'll fix your leg properly where I have equipment and decent light. I need to check for nerve damage.' But already he was checking toes and leg for response, and he was thinking Christopher had been lucky.

'But what about Ruby?' Maggie demanded

And he thought...*Ruby.*

Uh-oh. Ruby.

His baby?

She was not his baby, he told himself harshly. She was merely his responsibility until she could be evacuated or her mother reclaimed her. No more.

'Your sister's caring for her,' he told Maggie. 'In the car,' he added, and hoped she was.

'If she's with Liselle, she'll be fine,' Maggie assured him. 'Liselle loves babies. She makes money babysitting.' But she was frowning, obviously thinking ahead.

'Blake, Chris obviously needs careful stitching.' She glanced at the leg Blake had now bound so tightly the bleeding had completely stopped. 'I think...even if Christopher's okay with it, it might be too big a job to do here. I can cope with simple suturing, but this might need more. On top of that, Ruby's legs need attention. The sooner the pair of them get professional care, the better. Added to that, I don't want the responsibility for your appendix. The sensible plan is to organise evacuation for the three of you. I'll get the chopper in now—they'll fly you all over to the hospital.'

'I don't want to go to hospital,' Christopher whimpered, sounding panicked, and suddenly Blake was right there, concurring.

'I don't either,' he said. 'I can fix this.' He put a hand on Christopher's shoulder, settling him. 'I'm a surgeon and I do a neat job of stitching,' he said. 'No criticism of your sister but she's a girl. What do girls know abut needlework?'

That produced a faint smile on the boy's wan face. 'Yeah, right.'

'So it's okay if I put your leg back together instead of your sister? Without sending you to hospital?'

'Okay,' Christopher whispered, and Maggie hugged him.

Blake wondered why Maggie was doing the hugging instead of the wimp of a woman that was their mother.

'I'm going to make myself a nice cup of tea,' the woman was saying, staggering to her feet. 'I'm Barbie, by the way. Barbara, but my friends call me Barbie. Maggie, you might have introduced me.'

Right, Blake thought. Introductions before saving her son's life?

Christopher was slipping towards sleep. The saline was pushing his blood pressure up. The painkillers were taking effect. They had time to think this through but what he was suggesting—staying here—still seemed sensible.

Even to him.

'What about Ruby?' Maggie asked as her mother disappeared, jerking him back to his baby, his responsibility.

But responsibilities weren't only his. His thoughts were flying tangentially, from a wounded child to a baby—and to one lone nurse.

One look at this family and he'd seen what Maggie was facing. The mother was feeble and hysterical, the father was nowhere to be seen, and these kids were too young to be alone. Maggie seemed to be caring for everyone. More than that, she was taking on the medical needs for the entire population of this side of the valley. Until the water receded, she was on her own.

Christopher would live. If Maggie had been on her own, he might well not have. They both knew that. Maggie's white face told him she'd seen it and was still seeing it. But together they'd worked well. They'd worked as a team.

He was on leave. He needed to sort the house. How hard would it be to provide back-up for this woman?

And care for a baby while he did?

She'd help him with Ruby, he thought. Maggie was that sort of woman.

'No,' she said.

'No?'

Her eyes narrowed, and she made her voice resolute. 'I know what you're thinking and no. I'm *not* helping look after your baby and you *are* being evacuated.'

'I wasn't asking you to look after my…my sister's baby,' he said, and thought, Okay, he might have been going to suggest it but he wasn't now. 'And you don't need to look after my appendix. In case you hadn't realised it, most appendectomies result in removal of same, and I've left mine safely in Sydney.' Then, as she opened her mouth to protest some more, he held up his hand to pre-empt her.

'Plus,' he said, 'I was looked after by colleagues, medical mates who know they'll get joshed for ever if I'm hit by complications, so I have enough antibiotics on board to protect a horse. I'm healing nicely. Plus…' she'd opened her mouth again… 'if you send Ruby to hospital the first thing they'll do is to organise an orthopaedic surgeon opinion. I'm suspecting Corella

Valley doesn't run to an orthopaedic surgeon. The nearest orthopaedic surgeon would therefore be me, and I'm on this side of the river. Maggie, not only can I assess Ruby, I can manipulate and cast her legs. I can do everything she needs until the water comes down.'

'And look after her?'

'I… Yes,' he said, and he met her gaze full on. 'And Wendy knows where she is right now,' he said. 'She might change her mind. That option's not available if Ruby's sent to the city.'

'I doubt—'

'So do I doubt,' he said softly. 'But Wendy's my sister so maybe I should care for this little one for a week or two and give her that chance.'

'Would you want her to go back to…that?' she demanded, appalled.

'No,' he said truthfully. 'But I do want to talk to Wendy. I do want to figure this mess out. I don't want to walk away…'

'From your family,' she said, her voice softening.

'I've figured it,' he told her, glancing up at the roof. 'Risks are everywhere. If I turn my back, the next thing I know Ruby will be roof-sliding.'

'You'll take responsibility for her?'

'For a week or so,' he said, wondering what on earth he'd let himself in for. But there was something about this moment…something about the

way this woman was shouldering so much responsibility—that made him think, One baby for
a week. Was that a lot to ask?

Family for a week.

He could do this, he thought, and somehow…
maybe it'd be his only chance to make reparation
for a sister who'd never had a Maggie.

Why?

Because he'd thought of Wendy. For whatever
reason, he'd thought of that baby, glimpsed only
that once.

He hadn't had a great childhood, but many had
it worse. His mother had had enough strength to
walk away from her abusive husband. She hadn't
been a particularly affectionate mother but the
man she'd married next had been distantly kind.
Money had never been an issue. He'd gone to a
great school, to an excellent university.

Wendy, though…

He knew enough of his father to know there'd
have been no support for an illegitimate child.
He didn't know who her mother was, but he remembered hysteria, threats, floods of tears, and
he thought… He thought Wendy must have had
the worst side of the deal by far.

You've got the farm… She'd thrown that at him
as an accusation.

Did he have the right to accept it? For the first
time he was questioning it.

Maggie was watching him. Waiting for him to realise what he was letting himself in for. Waiting for him to realise that evacuation was the easiest way to go.

But then he thought back to that moment all those years ago. Seeing a child… Thinking for one amazing moment that he had a little sister.

Family.

He didn't do family. He was a loner. Miriam was all he needed—a woman as caught up in her career as he was in his.

Miriam would think he was nuts.

'Hey, mister, I think your baby's filled her nappy. You want me to change it? I can but I charge babysitting rates.' It was a yell from the far side of the house and it jerked him out of introspection as nothing else could have. It even made him smile.

'He's coming, Liselle,' Maggie said. She was cradling Christopher, hugging him close, surveying Blake like he was an interesting insect species. She was watching to see what he'd do. 'There's no need for him to waste money employing nappy-changers, and there are no nappy-changers available for hire anyway. There are nappies in my bag,' she told him. 'Or there's still the choice of evacuation. What's it to be?'

And he looked down at Christopher—who'd need to be evacuated with him—that wound needed careful stitching and it was too much to expect Maggie to do it. He looked at Maggie, who'd taken on responsibility for the valley.

He thought about Ruby, whose need had just graphically been described.

'I guess I'm staying,' he said, and Maggie smiled up at him. It wasn't a confident smile, though. Maybe she still thought he'd be more trouble than he was worth.

'You're a brave man,' she told him. 'Changing nappies isn't for sissies.'

'Then I guess I can't be a sissy,' he told her, grinning back at her. Thinking this could be a very interesting week. Thinking Here Be Dragons but he could just possibly tackle them and do this woman a favour in the process. 'I can't be a sissy until the floods subside.'

'Or until after you've coped with one nappy,' Maggie said. 'Nappy or floods...take your pick.'

'I have a feeling I'm facing both.'

They tucked Christopher into the back seat of Maggie's wagon. It was a tight fit around the baby seat but they stuffed the leg space with cushions so he could lie down, they wrapped him in blankets and he settled. It wasn't only the drugs that made him relax, Maggie thought. Whenever one of the kids was ill it was 'We want Maggie.' More, it was 'We *need* Maggie.' And they did.

She slid behind the steering-wheel, checked on her now sleeping little brother, an awake but changed and clean Ruby—and one recovering appendectomy patient beside her.

Mother hen with all her chicks.

Blake wasn't quite a chick.

He was staying.

She should be relieved. She was relieved. He'd been brilliant with Christopher. She might have got the bleeding checked in time, but she might not have. The odds said not. She glanced again at Christopher and her heart twisted.

She glanced at Blake—and something inside twisted in a different direction.

Weird?

Yes, it was weird. This guy was a doctor, a surgeon. He was here to help and she should be overjoyed, in a purely professional capacity. But there was a little bit of her that wasn't professional, which was reacting to the sense of this guy sitting beside her, which was saying that Blake deciding to stay might cause problems...

What problems? She was being ridiculous. It was the shock of what had just happened, she told herself firmly. It was the shock of almost losing one of her family.

She loved the lot of them. All eight. They held her heartstrings and she was tied for life.

So put the weird way she was feeling about Blake right away—forget it.

'Why did you decide to leave them?' Blake asked and she concentrated on the road for a while, concentrated on getting her thoughts in order, concentrated on suppressing anger and confusion and whatever else was whirling in her traitorous mind.

'You think I should still be living with them?'

'I don't think,' Blake said mildly. 'But I'm wondering if your father's a bit more capable than your mother.'

'He's not,' she said shortly. 'And he doesn't live there any more.'

'I'm sorry.'

'I'm not,' she said. 'It's one less responsibility.' Then she caught herself. 'Sorry. That sounds like they're all hard work. They're great kids. Nickie, Louise and Raymond have scholarships and are at university. Donny's in his last year as an apprentice motor mechanic. They're all safe.'

'How did you train?' he asked, mildly, thinking if she had been responsible for them all...had she left and come back?

'Luck,' she said briefly. 'Dad was restless and moved us all to Cairns. It was dumb—we knew no one there and ended up reliant on Social Services but it took four years to get enough money together to come back, so I was able to do my basic nursing training while I lived with them. Otherwise I'd be stuck with nothing.'

'Stuck with your family?'

'That's it,' she said quietly. 'And it's a quandary. The kids love me and need me, but they're growing up. Gradually they're making their way into the world, so I need to work out my own independence as well. I know I have eventual escape, but Liselle, Peter, Christopher and Susie are seventeen, fifteen, twelve and ten and too young to be left with the cot case that's my mother. But I didn't have a choice—until your father's farm became available.'

'You're saying you left your family to take care of my father's farm?'

'I left my family for me,' she said grimly, and there was a moment's silence while she obviously decided whether to reveal more of herself. And came down on the yes side.

'My dad left two years ago,' she told him. 'He's as bad as my mum. Totally irresponsible. Six months ago, just as your dad was dying, he turned up with a new young partner in tow. Sashabelle. What sort of name is that? Anyway they giggled and mooned over each other and Sashabelle kept saying how cute Susie was and how she'd love to have a daughter—all in my mother's hearing— and then Dad looked at me and grinned and said to her, "Yeah, sweetheart, you know I love travelling but if you really want a kid…if worst comes to worst we can always bring her home to Maggie.'"

'And I thought that's exactly what would happen. Just like Wendy's dumped Ruby on you—only I've already cared for eight and I'm d— I'm darned if I'll look after more. So I told him no more, ever, I was moving out. Then I had to find somewhere where I could reach the kids in a hurry when they need me, but my useless parents know that I've drawn a line and any more kids—no way. Once Susie's left home, I'm out of it. Good ole Maggie… I love my brothers and sisters to bits but the end's in sight.'

'So that's why you won't take on Ruby?'

Her face froze. 'No,' she said through gritted teeth. 'It's not why I won't take on Ruby. I'm not taking on Ruby because she's not my family, and it's totally, crassly, cruelly irresponsible for you to ask it of me. I'm your tenant, Blake, but if babies are involved you won't see me for dust. Put that in your pipe and smoke it—and don't forget it. And here we are.'

They'd pulled into the grounds of the local hall. A dumpy little lady in her forties was tacking a banner to the fence.

Medical Clinic, Temporary, Corella Valley East.

A sign hung on a nail in front of it.

'*Maggie's Not Here.*'

As Maggie swung into the gate the lady at the fence beamed, waved and swapped the sign over.

'*Maggie's Here.*'

'Very professional,' Blake said dryly, and Maggie cast him a wry look.

'So how would you organise it, city boy?'

'Regular hours?'

'And when another kid falls off a roof I still stay here because I need to be regular? I'll be here when I can.' She climbed out of the car and hugged the lady doing the signs. 'Ronnie, this looks great. Fantastic. And we have our first patient. Christopher.'

Ronnie sighed and tugged away to look into the back seat. 'Oh, Christopher, what have you done now?' And then she paused as Blake emerged from the passenger seat. 'Oh…'

'This is Blake Samford,' Maggie said briefly. 'He's Bob's son—and a doctor. He's offered to help. Blake, this is Veronica Mayes. Ronnie. She's a schoolteacher, but the school's on the other side of the river.'

'You're a doctor.' Ronnie's eyes grew huge. 'A medical doctor—here? On this side. Oh, Maggie, that's wonderful.' She peered again into the back seat. 'But Christopher…?'

'Sliding on roof ended badly,' Maggie said

curtly. 'Badly cut thigh. It needs stitching and Blake's offered to help.'

'And…the baby?' She was still staring into the car.

'Ruby,' Maggie said. 'Blake's baby. If he asks nicely, he might be persuade you to take care of her while he stitches.'

'You've brought your family here?' Ronnie demanded of Blake, beaming her excitement.

'Just his baby,' Maggie said. 'I suspect Blake thinks that's enough.'

The wound on Christopher's leg was jagged and bone deep. He was incredibly lucky to have escaped nerve damage, Blake thought as he cleaned, debrided and inserted internal stitches as well as external to hold everything together. They'd sedated the boy heavily, so he wasn't out of it completely but he was wafting in a drug-induced haze. Maggie was doing the reassurance, prattling on about some weird video game Christopher loved, but at the same time she was giving him every inch of assistance he needed.

She was an excellent nurse, Blake thought. The valley was lucky to have her.

As he started the final suturing and dressing, Ronnie poked her head round the door and said apologetically, 'Maggie, love, Joan Kittle's here with Angus with asthma.'

'I can handle Angus's asthma,' Maggie told Blake. 'Mild asthmatic, hysterical mum.'

'There seems to be an abundance of hysterical mothers in this valley,' he noted, keeping on working. 'Christopher, is it okay if your sister goes out to take care of a child with asthma?'

'Yeah,' Christopher said sleepily. 'You'll look after me, and everyone always needs Maggie.'

They did. He had that pretty much figured by now.

He finished stitching and dressing and tucked the little boy under blankets. Ronnie appeared again with a sleepy Ruby in her arms. He asked her to stay with Christopher and went to find out what was happening.

Angus was obviously sorted. Maggie was now examining a toe, attached to a very large, very elderly guy who looked like he'd just come in from the cowshed. He sat slumped in a rather rickety chair in the makeshift waiting room, his boot off and his foot stuck straight out in front of him.

Maggie turned as he entered and he was hit by a smile of sheer, anticipatory gratitude.

'Mr Bowen has a splinter,' she said.

'Went out to chop the wood in me slippers,' the old man said. 'Dumb. Coulda chopped me foot off with an axe. Didn't. Hit the wood with the splitter, though, and a bit of wood went right in. I've been digging round all morning with a needle and can't get it. Maggie says you're a doc.'

He was an orthopaedic surgeon, Blake thought faintly. Was he supposed to go digging for splinters?

But that's what he did. He inserted local anaesthetic. He did a part resection of the nail of the big toe and managed the careful removal of a shattered splinter.

He administered a decent shot of antibiotics—the guy had indeed been digging into the wound and Blake hated to imagine what he'd used to do it. He added a tetanus booster and a dressing and the man was ready to heave himself up and leave—but not before commenting on what had happened and on who Blake was.

'Bob's son, eh?' he said jovially. 'You sure don't take after your old man. I can't see Bob Samford pulling splinters out of anyone's toes—he'd be more likely driving them in. And Ronnie tells me you're here with your daughter. How about that? A whole new generation for Corella Valley Homestead. I'll tell the wife to bake a cake.'

And before Blake had a chance to rebut or even answer, he was hit by a slap on the back that made him stagger and the guy was gone.

Leaving him…speechless.

Blake Samford returns to the family property with daughter…

Not so much.

Maggie was cleaning up. She had her back to him. She didn't say a word.

He wanted to see her expression. He badly wanted to see her expression.

She'd better not be laughing.

'All finished,' Ronnie asked, opening the door so they could see through to Christopher. 'Chris wants to go home. Is he going back to your mum, Maggie, or will you take him back with you?'

'He'll need to come with me,' Maggie said doubtfully. 'Mum won't keep him quiet.'

'Then you'll need Liselle,' Ronnie decreed. She eyed Blake thoughtfully while she spoke, obviously planning ahead. 'At seventeen Liselle's more than competent to do some babysitting,' she told Blake. 'And she'll love getting away from her mother's weird music so she can do some serious study. Unless *you're* happy to stay home all the time.' She arched her eyebrows at Blake, and grinned.

'That's exactly what Blake should be doing,' Maggie retorted. 'He's recovering from appendicitis.'

'Really?' Ronnie was bug-eyed. 'You've come home to recover? Isn't that nice.'

'I've come home... I've come *back* to put the farm on the market,' he growled, and she grinned.

'That sounds more like your dad. But you're

going to be useful while you do it, which isn't like your dad at all. So... Christopher and Liselle... they won't fit in that tiny apartment of yours, Maggie.'

'Christopher can share my bed. You know we do that when any of them are ill. Liselle can sleep on the sofa.'

'I've seen your sofa,' Ronnie said darkly. 'Charity-shop reject if ever I saw one. Poor Liselle.' Then she looked—archly—at Blake. 'Your house, though, has more bedrooms—and more beds— than you can poke a stick at. If you're going to be useful, why not be properly useful? Let Liselle and Christopher stay in your part of the house. Maggie won't even go through your door except to dust, and it's always seemed such a waste.'

'Ronnie,' Maggie snapped. 'You know—'

'I know you've made a huge effort to get away from your family and I know why,' Ronnie said. 'But this wouldn't be you taking them in. It'd be Dr Blake taking them in, in exchange for Liselle occasionally looking after his baby. She can't get to school but she needs to study. I suspect she'll get more study done at your place than at your mother's.' Then, as Maggie looked doubtful, she said, more gently, 'Surely your mum can cope with just Peter and Susie?'

'I guess...' Maggie said slowly. 'I worry about Pete—those mates of his are wild but he has two new computer games he's obsessed with, and he's promised… And Susie'll be fine. She spends her time with the little girl next door. But—'

'Then there you are,' Ronnie said, beaming, refusing to listen to buts. 'Problem solved. Corella Homestead will have two adults and three kids. It's built for more but it's a start.'

'Ronnie, it's Blake's house.'

'But he's helping,' Ronnie said, pseudo innocent. 'It's a flood. Everyone helps in a flood. Isn't that right, Dr Samford?'

Open his house up, Blake thought, floundering. To three kids and one nurse? This hadn't been in the contract when he'd taken Maggie in as a tenant.

The house was built for more.

He thought of the house as he remembered it, exquisitely furnished by his mother. It still was, even though the furnishings were long faded. She'd set up all the bedrooms for guests who'd never come—one hint of his father's temper had been enough to drive them away.

He had five bedrooms, plus the tiny apartment that was Maggie's.

What harm in letting them be used?

Letting a family into his life…

Don't be dramatic, he told himself harshly, and another voice in his head said it would diffuse the situation. He wouldn't be stuck with one baby. He didn't need to bond. With a house full of people Ruby would be just one more.

'She's starting to fret,' Ronnie told him, and before he could demur she'd handed Ruby over, an armful of needy baby. 'Get out of here. Go home and feed your baby. Maggie, your wagon's full. You want me to go and fetch Liselle and bring the kids' gear over?'

'Blake hasn't even said yes yet,' Maggie said, a trifle desperately, and Ronnie put her hands on her hips and fixed him with a schoolmarm look.

'He hasn't either,' she said. 'So what's it to be, Dr Samford? Do you want me to fetch Liselle, or can you look after your baby all by yourself? She does babysitting for pocket money. She's studying for her university entrance exams. She has Maggie for a sister. She's good.'

'But Maggie herself…' he said, feeling helpless.

'Maggie's busy,' Ronnie snapped, glancing at Maggie. 'It's Liselle or nothing. And you might be generous. You don't have to be like your father, you know.'

'That's blackmail,' Maggie retorted, and Ronnie grinned.

'I know but it's working. Look at his face.'

And of course it was. *You don't have to be like your father…*

It was a powerful statement.

The valley was flooded. These were emergency conditions. A man had to pull his weight.

By letting a family into his life?

He didn't do family.

He was holding family in his arms.

'Fine,' he said, and Ronnie's grin widened.

'That's very gracious. You might say fine and mean it. Liselle's lovely and almost as competent as her sister. Christopher's fun. Maggie's magnificent. You're getting a very good deal, Dr Samford.'

'Fine,' he repeated, but this time he managed a weak smile. 'Let's do it.' He met Maggie's gaze and for the first time he realised she was looking almost as trapped as he was.

She was Maggie the magnificent, he thought—who also didn't do family. Or who didn't want to. She was Maggie who was more trapped than he was.

'Fine,' he said for the third time. 'We can do this, can't we, Maggie? For a week or so... For a week or so we can put up with anything.'

CHAPTER FIVE

BEFORE they left the clinic Blake took basic X-rays of Ruby's legs—enough to confirm what he needed to know. Then they went back to the homestead, with Blake taking what he needed with him.

Ruby's feet needed urgent attention. The X-rays showed there was no underlying complication, but at birth the tissues were soft and pliable and every day that passed meant manipulation would be harder and the treatment longer. By six months she'd be facing surgery, but at three weeks of age there was still time for the feet to be manoeuvred into the right position.

Maggie settled Christopher and Liselle into the bedrooms closest to her part of the house. He listened to their amazement at the opulence of his parents' former life while he did what he'd needed to since last night.

He did a careful, thorough examination of Ruby's feet.

A full CT scan of her feet would be good, but

that meant evacuation. He could scarcely justify using emergency services when he felt sure the X-rays had shown enough. But there were other factors at play. If he accepted evacuation with Ruby and he went with her, it seemed a statement that he wasn't ready to make. That she somehow belonged to him. But if he didn't leave with her, if he sent her away on her own, that meant welfare. Foster-parents. Losing control.

No. Not yet. For some strange reason he was starting to feel that, whatever this little girl's future was, he wanted a say in it.

Since last night he'd been holding her, feeding her, cradling her, and somehow she was starting to change him. She was starting to make him feel as he'd never expected to feel.

He and Miriam had never talked about having children. Children weren't on their horizon. Now, though, as he held Ruby, as he felt her tiny head nuzzle into the crook of his neck, searching for the security of his warmth and his strength, he felt his world shift a little.

The thought kept coming back…the memory of the tiny girl he'd seen once when he'd been six years old.

She'd been wailing and he'd wanted to do something. He'd wanted to shout at the adults to stop fighting and make the baby better.

He hadn't realised it had had such an impact,

but now, all these years later, this baby was in his hands, and maybe he could help this time.

To make her better?

Maggie had thrust this baby at him. She expected him to help.

She wasn't with him now. She was caught up settling Christopher, but it felt like she was right here, watching.

Judging?

Do no harm. That was the first principle of medicine. He examined the X-rays and was satisfied. He carefully manipulated Ruby's tiny, twisted feet and he grew more and more certain that this was straight congenital talipes equinovarus, with no other factors coming into play.

There was no major deformity—it had just been the way she'd lain in utero, her feet twisted and gradually setting in a position that, if left untreated, would cause lifelong problems.

He'd set her on Maggie's cashmere rug in the middle of his bed. She'd just been fed but she wasn't asleep. It almost seemed like she was enjoying him playing with her feet, gently massaging, gently manipulating.

Her eyes were huge. She was up to focussing, but not smiling. He thought, though, that she was almost there.

He was examining her feet but he was also trying to make her smile.

'Five weeks,' Maggie said from the door, and he started like he'd been caught stealing. Trying to steal a smile?

'What…?'

'Babies are generally five weeks old until you can reliably say the smile's not wind. But not your baby, of course.' She grinned. 'Every parent thinks their baby's far, far smarter and it's not wind at all. So what's the prognosis?'

Every parent…

The words hung. He should refute them. He did, in his head, but he didn't say it out loud.

It was something to do with the way Ruby was looking up at him. The contact was fleetingly— her focus was short lived—but he had established eye contact.

Part of him wanted to say, *I am not this child's parent*, but to do that when he'd been trying to make her smile…

'They twist your heartstrings, don't they?' Maggie said gently. 'Family. I have Christopher next door. He's settling to sleep and my heart's only just beginning to beat again.'

And Christopher was twelve, Blake thought. Twelve years of heartstrings. And for Maggie that was multiplied by eight.

He couldn't begin to comprehend that sort of commitment.

'Will the other two be okay with their mother? Pete and Susie?'

'You mean should I bring them here, too?' she asked wryly. 'Um, no. Mum'd come then, too, and Dad and his girlfriend might well decide why not come as well, and where would you be then?'

He stopped looking at Ruby. He looked... stunned. How many Tildens?

'Don't worry,' she told him, and grinned. 'Your dad did you a favour. The whole district knows the Samfords are mean and grumpy. I doubt Mum'll dare to come close—she doesn't care enough about Christopher to try. But she's not a terrible mother, if that's what you're worrying about. She doesn't drink or belt the kids. She just goes about making dandelion tea or goat's-milk balm or practising her latest yoga moves while the kids do what they like. I think they'll be safe enough—and I'm here as back-up.'

'So I don't get your whole family under my roof?'

'Heaven forbid,' she said, quite lightly but he could hear a whole depth of emotion behind those words. 'So you're tackling Ruby's feet. Do you want help?'

And here she was again, practical Maggie, moving in to do what was necessary—and then moving out again.

He was starting to see, very clearly, exactly

how and why those boundaries had been put in place.

'I brought back the things I need,' he told her.

'I saw you collecting them from the clinic. Like what?'

'The makings for casts,' he told her, going back to massaging the little girl's feet. 'I'm sure this is straightforward congenital talipes. See how I can move them? It's not causing her pain when I manipulate—the tissue's still incredibly pliable. The trick is to get the feet into the right position before we lose that pliability. Which is now.

'What we do is manipulate the feet back as far as we can, then apply casts. We leave the casts on for a week, then remove them and do the same thing again. We're inching her feet into correct position. The majority of cases can be corrected in six to eight weeks. Before we apply the last plaster cast we'll probably need to cut the Achilles tendons—an Achilles tenotomy—but that's a small procedure, nothing like the drama of a torn Achilles tendon in an adult. But that's weeks away.'

'You mean…she'll be cured within a few weeks?'

'They'll be back in position then, but if left they'll revert. She'll need to wear a brace for twenty-three hours a day for three months and then at night-time for three to four years. She may end up with slightly smaller feet than she otherwise would, and her feet might not be exactly the same size, but by the time she goes to school she'll be essentially normal.'

'Wow,' Maggie breathed. 'That's awesome. I learned about talipes in training but I've never seen it. I was imagining disability for life.'

'I imagine that's what Wendy thought, too,' Blake said grimly.

'Are you going to tell her?' She hesitated. 'You know, if Wendy thought she had a normal baby girl she might not have abandoned her.'

'I've thought of that.'

He'd also thought… He could phone her. Come and get your daughter because she's normal.

He raked his hair and thought about it some more. He looked down at his niece and he thought…

Deformed rat. The vindictiveness of what had been said. The bruise on her shoulder. And Wendy hadn't stood up for her.

'Not yet,' he said, and it came out harshly. 'Let's see if she misses her first.'

She'd have to make some effort, he thought. Make some contact. For him to hand this little one back to a pair who'd tossed her aside…

'You're falling in love with her,' Maggie said on a note of discovery and he thought…he thought…

Actually, he thought nothing. The statement left him stunned, like all the air had been sucked from the room.

Love.

What sort of statement was that?

He gazed down at the baby and while he he was looking at her thought he saw a tiny flicker of a smile.

'Wind,' Maggie said.

'It was a smile.'

'See,' Maggie said, and grinned. 'Parents.'

The air disappeared again. Parents. Family.

'So what do we do?' Maggie said, and there was another word.

We.

It made what was happening less terrifying, he thought.

'If you're happy to help…'

'Of course I am.'

'Unless I ask for babysitting.'

'That's not my job and you know it's not—Doctor,' she said primly. 'Let's keep this professional. So what's the plan?

If she was to be professional, so could he. He looked down at those tiny feet and thought of what had to be done.

'The first manipulation aims to raise the first metatarsal, decreasing the cavus,' he told her, thinking it through as he spoke. 'We'll apply long leg casts to hold everything in position after the manipulation. You had everything we needed back in the clinic. Are you treating greenstick fractures yourself?'

'Hopefully not, but if I have to I will. We can't depend on evacuation. That's why the X-ray machine.'

'It's great for us that it's there. It makes me confident of what we're dealing with, and I can feel pretty much what I need to feel now. We'll get the feet into position and in casts. In a week we take them off. The next manipulations involve abduction of the forefoot with counter-pressure on the neck of the talus. Carefully. You don't pronate— and you never put counter-pressure on the calcaneus or the cuboid.'

'I promise I won't,' she said—and she grinned. 'Doctor. Whatever calcaneus or cuboids are. Wow, isn't Ruby lucky to have an orthopod as an uncle?'

'I wouldn't call Ruby lucky,' he said grimly.

'I don't know,' Maggie said, suddenly thoughtful. 'If you'd told me a week ago that being born into the Samford family was lucky I'd have said you had rocks in your head—for all this place is worth a fortune. But now...I'm seeing a seriously different Samford and I'm impressed.'

'Don't be,' he growled. 'I'm out of here in a week.'

'So you're being nice for a week?'

'Until the bridge is safe.'

'Well, then,' Maggie said briskly, 'tell me what you need to do and we'll start doing it. If Ruby and I only have a week of niceness, we'd best make the most of it.'

The procedure to manipulate and cast Ruby's legs was straightforward enough, but it was also enough to show Maggie that in Blake she had a seriously skilled operator.

This was one tiny baby. His fingers were as gentle as a mother's, fingering the tiny toes, carefully, gently massaging, moving, wiggling, taking all the time in the world so Ruby felt no pain. Instead she seemed to be enjoying it, lying back on pillows, wide awake, seemingly savouring the sensation of this big man caressing her twisted legs, playing with her—and smiling at her while he did it.

He'd be a good surgeon, Maggie thought with sudden perception. If she were an old lady with a broken hip, she'd like it to be this man treating her. She thought suddenly, Samford or not, this smile was not just for this baby.

He'd used it on Christopher who, terrifyingly reckless at the best of times, was usually a total wimp when it came to doctors and needles. Christopher was tucked up in bed, happy and safe, because of this man.

Ruby was having her legs encased in casts and she looked not the least bit perturbed. She looked as if she had total trust in Blake as well.

In a Samford.

In a man no one knew anything about.

Maggie reminded herself of that, over and over, as she handed Blake what he needed, as she held the little legs in position as Blake wound the dressings, as she watched as he took the first steps to make this little girl perfect.

And she thought… Uh-oh.

This was one sexy male, and there weren't a lot of sexy males in Maggie's orbit. She needed to keep a clear head and remember—this guy was a Samford. Son of the local squattocracy. She was a Tilden. Daughter of the local welfare bludgers.

As well as that, he was here for a week. She was here for life.

So she'd better stop what she was thinking right now, she told herself. Just because the man had the sexiest, most skilful hands and was smiling at Ruby with a smile to make a girl's toes curl…

Maggie couldn't understand why Ruby wasn't beaming back—but a girl had to keep her feet firmly on the ground and remember relative positions in the world. This guy was her landlord and she needed to stay professional and get back to her side of the wall, *now*.

But Liselle and Christopher were on this side of the wall and Blake would need her advice with Ruby so she'd be on his side of the wall at other times, and boundaries were blurring.

It was up to her to keep them in place—and stop looking at this guy's smile!

By the time they were finished, Ruby was fast asleep. So much for a traumatic medical procedure. She was snuggled on her pillows, dead to the world, sucking her fist and totally, absolutely contented with her lot.

As Maggie cleared the remains of the dressings, Blake looked down at his niece as if he didn't quite know what to do next.

'How about sleep?' Maggie suggested, and he looked at her like he'd forgotten she was there.

'She's already asleep.'

'You,' she said gently. 'Appendicitis. Recovery. I just bet your surgeon said get lots of rest.'

'He might have.' It was a grudging admission.

'Then sleep.'

'I need to move her,' he said, sounding helpless, and she grinned.

Ruby was on the left side of the bed. She took two pillows and tucked them against the edge so even if Ruby managed a roll—pretty much impossible at three weeks—she'd go nowhere.

'That leaves you the whole right-hand side of

the bed,' she said. 'She'll sleep better knowing you're close. Babies sense these things.'

'Nonsense.'

It might be nonsense, Maggie thought, but she wasn't telling this guy that. What she was aiming for—what Ruby needed more than anything in the world—was for someone—anyone—to bond with her. To bond so tightly that they'd fight for her for life.

'There's lots of room for both of you,' she said briskly. 'Bed. Now! Would you like me to bring you a cup of tea? Toast?'

'No,' he said, sounding revolted. 'I'm not a patient.'

'But you're not fully healed,' she told him. 'And I'm treating you like the goose that lays the golden eggs. In you I have a qualified surgeon on my side of the river and there's no way I'm planning on letting you have a relapse. Bed. Now. Egg on toast, coming up.

'Maggie?'

'Yes' she said, and raised an enquiring brow—like an old-fashioned matron faced with an impertinent patient who should know better than to question her medical edicts.

'Never mind,' he said, and she grinned.

'Good boy. You just hop into bed with your baby and let Nurse Maggie judge what's best.'

And how was a man to respond to that?

* * *

Everyone seemed headed for a nap. Even Liselle had been shaken enough by the morning's events to want to snooze. She'd brought books to study but she was ensconced in one of Corella View's gorgeous, if faded, guest rooms, she had an entire double bed to herself and she couldn't resist.

'This place is fabulous, Mags,' she whispered as she snuggled into an ancient feather eiderdown and a pile of goosedown pillows. 'I could stay here for ever.'

'Blake's selling the house and he'll be gone in a week,' Maggie said, a bit too waspishly, and Liselle looked up at her in concern.

'Does that upset you?'

'I… No.'

'It means you'll come home to us,' Liselle said sleepily. 'That's good. I like sharing my bedroom with you.'

Maggie smiled at her—but she didn't mean that smile. Going home to her family…

But where else could she live in this valley that wasn't home? Blake had been charging her peppercorn rent in return for caring for the house and dogs. She was a mile away from her family, and that was about the extent of safe range. Today had proved that.

She left her sister to sleep, made herself tea and toast and went out to sit on the veranda.

It was starting to rain again.

She was sick to death of rain.

She was sick to death of this valley.

Actually, it wasn't true. She loved the valley. Her parents' time in the city had been a nightmare and she'd returned home with them feeling nothing but relief.

But she wanted to be free.

What would it be like, she wondered, to spend a couple of weeks lying on a beach somewhere it wasn't raining? Somewhere all by herself?

It couldn't happen. The kids needed all her spare income for their schoolbooks and extra expenses. The welfare payments her mother received could only go so far. They depended on her.

So no holidays for Maggie.

So you might as well quit whinging, she told herself, and glanced back at Blake's bedroom window as though he might have heard the thought.

She hoped he was asleep.

Her cellphone beeped. She checked it and winced. Old Ron Macy from up on the ridge had fallen and his ulcerated leg was bleeding. She needed to go.

But at least she had support. Blake was here, with Liselle as back-up.

She didn't even need to tell him she was leaving, she thought, and she thought back to last night, to Blake calmly handing over the baby to her. *Here you are, your problem.*

She couldn't help grinning. She could go now, and the whole household would be *his* problem.

Blackie was restless. The dogs had learned by now that the phone usually meant she had to go. He was whining and she knew why. She rubbed his ears and then she tiptoed through the house to Blake's bedroom and stealthily unlatched the door to Blake's bedroom. Thunderstorms were due. The forecast was horrendous, and Blackie was probably already hearing thunder in the distance.

If storms hit in earnest Blake would find himself with two dogs on his bed—or under his bed—but it'd be better than them turning themselves inside out with fear.

She was leaving Blake with baby and dogs and her siblings.

He was recovering from an appendectomy.

'He's a big boy,' she said, hardening her heart, but she didn't have to harden it too much. Blake was snuggled in bed while she had to brave the elements.

And then she thought she didn't mind this. A house full of people where she didn't have responsibility.

It was sort of like a holiday, she told herself—only different.

* * *

Blake woke up and Ruby was wailing, two dogs had their noses in his face and two wan kids were huddled in the doorway.

And the sky was falling.

Okay, it wasn't quite, but that's what it sounded like. It was either dusk or the storm was so bad the light had disappeared—the natural light, that was, because the lightning was almost one continuous sheet. There was no gap between the lightning and thunder. The rain was pounding so hard on the roof it almost felt as if the house itself was vibrating.

He must have been tired to have slept until now, but suddenly he was wide awake. Wet dog noses would do that to you. Both the dogs were shivering wrecks. The next bout of thunder boomed, and Ruby's cry turned to a yell—and the kids from the door saw he was awake and suddenly they were right in bed with him.

Dogs, too. Why not? This was a huddle of quivering terror and he was in the middle.

'Um…it's just a thunderstorm, guys,' he managed, trying to wake up, and in response they cringed closer. He moved over and lifted Chris nearer so his bandaged leg wasn't squashed. With Ruby on the other side of him he was practically a Blake sandwich. 'You should be in your own beds.'

'We don't like thunderstorms,' Liselle said. 'And Maggie's gone.'

Gone. For one appalling moment he had visions of Maggie doing what Ruby's parents had done—cutting and running. Heading over the threatened bridge, taking off for Queensland, leaving him with Ruby and Christopher and Liselle and Blackie and Tip.

'There….there's a note on the kitchen table,' Liselle quavered. 'Mr Macy on the ridge has fallen over and she had to go up and put a dressing on his leg. She says she'll be back by teatime but if I'm worried about Christopher then talk to you.'

'You shouldn't be worried,' Christopher said, not very stoutly. 'I'm okay.'

Except he was scared and he was hurting, Blake thought wryly. He shouldn't have tried bearing weight on that leg.

'The dogs are scared, too,' Liselle whispered, and the dogs whimpered in response. Blackie edged closer, edging around Christopher, her ancient nose pushing his chest—and suddenly she got what she wanted. The bedclothes were pushed back a bit and she was right down the foot of the bed so she was a mound of dog, like a wombat in a burrow, nestled hard against his feet.

Christopher giggled.

Ruby's wails grew louder.

Way back in Sydney, a really long time ago, Blake had wondered what he should do during his enforced convalescence. He had an excellent apartment with views over the harbour. Miriam was there in the evenings. He had a housekeeper to keep the place in order—everything he wanted. More. There were other medics—colleagues—in his apartment block and he wasn't left alone. His mates dropped in at all hours—*just to keep you company.* The decision to come here had been made partly for practical reasons but also because for some reason he was craving privacy.

Privacy had always been an issue for him. He'd learned early, in his parents' conflicted household, to disappear into his own world, and as an only child, even when his mother had remarried someone more reasonable, he'd known he'd been expected to fade into the background.

Isolation kept him out of emotional drama. It was a defence. Maybe that's why he and Miriam got on so well together—they instinctively respected personal space.

But he'd been at the same hospital for eight years now and lots of his colleagues no longer respected that space. Hence he'd decided that coming here was an option.

'I…I'll make Ruby's bottle, shall I?' Liselle quavered, and he looked at the slight seventeen-year-old who was obviously just as nervous as her brother.

'I'll get it,' he said, and swung back the covers, dislodging Tip in the process, who cast him a look of reproach. Then the next thunderclap boomed and the dog was down under the covers with Blackie.

'Maggie said you had to rest,' Liselle said.

'I'll rest. I'll get the bottle first.'

'And then you'll come back to us?'

To us. To a bed that was big but was now decidedly crowded. Two kids, two dogs, one baby.

'Yes,' he said, goaded.

'Maggie should be here,' Christopher whispered.

'Maggie wouldn't fit,' he retorted. 'You lie still and don't move that leg.' And then he went to fill his niece's very vocally broadcast requirements.

Maggie was heading home, feeling guilty.

So what was new? She'd felt guilty all her life. From the time her mother had made it very clear she needed her, anything Maggie had ever wanted to do for herself had been wasted time.

Now…she'd sort of wanted to stay in the big house and play with one baby and watch one guy bond with that baby, but she'd had no choice but to head up the valley to see Roy Macy. His leg was a mess but there was no way he'd come to her. His neighbour would have driven him but she knew exactly how he'd respond. 'No, don't fuss, leave it be.'

Left alone it'd turn into a septic mess, so good old Maggie had headed out into the storm and fixed it.

And left Blake with her responsibilities.

No. Ruby was his responsibility.

Why did it feel like she was hers?

Because she was used to feeling guilty. She'd sort of wanted to stay—but she'd felt guilty about leaving.

'I should have loaded Christopher into the car with me,' she said out loud. 'Just so I wouldn't feel like this.'

But she still would have. Guilt was unavoidable. Baby Ruby had crept round her heart like a small, needful worm and no matter how much she told herself she was nothing to do with her, she knew it wasn't true.

'It's only until the river level drops,' she told herself, looking bleakly out into the driving rain. 'Then they're out of here. I don't know what he'll do with Ruby, but it's not my problem. Not My Problem. Blake Samford is on his own. Just let the rain stop. Just let the river drop before I fall any deeper for one baby...'

And for the man who went with her?

'I'm not attached to Blake,' she said, astonished

at the places her thoughts were taking her. 'As if. Yes, he's gorgeous, but as if I have time...'

Time to notice how gorgeous he was?

She'd noticed.

She did not have time. She did not have the inclination.

Liar. Of course she had the inclination, only what chance was there ever for a love life for her when there were still four kids almost totally dependent on her?

'You'll start singing sad love songs next,' she told herself dryly. 'It's just the way things are. Get over it. And stop thinking of Blake Samford's body. Blake Samford's smile. Blake Samford's hands as he cradles his tiny niece...'

Whoa.

'The sooner the river drops the better for all concerned,' she muttered, and then she paused.

The thunder had been booming almost continuously since she'd left home and it was still booming, but over the noise she could hear...something else.

It was a roar, building from maybe imagined to real, growing more real by the moment.

Instinctively she swung the car away from the river road, up the slope of the valley.

To a place where she could see the massive force of water bursting down the valley as the dam upstream gave way.

To a place where she could see the bridge disappear in a maelstrom of rushing water, and the shallow slopes of the valley disappear within it.

CHAPTER SIX

'THE heifers…'

Blake was still in bed. He'd heard the bridge go. One part of him thought he should go and investigate the noise. The other part thought this farm was high and safe, he'd just got Ruby to sleep, the kids were settled, and there wasn't a lot he could do about a collapsing bridge.

Until Maggie burst in.

'The dam's burst upstream,' she said. She sounded exhausted, as though she'd run. She was soaking, her shirt was almost transparent, her curls were dripping round her shoulders, and the drips were making a puddle around her. 'Your heifers are trapped.'

'*My* heifers?' He didn't get it.

'Your calves,' she snapped. 'Your dad's yearlings. The water's come up too fast. I thought the bridge might go but not the dam. They're in the paddock on the far side of the road from the river, but the road's now under water. So's most of their paddock. There's a rise in the middle but it only holds half a dozen and the rest are already being forced to swim. If I can get them away from the rise, I can drive them to higher ground, but all they can see is the stupid island that's only going to let six or so survive. Liselle can't swim. She's scared of deep water and no one else is close enough to help. I know you're recovering but I don't have a choice. We can't let them drown. I need your help and I need it now.'

With Liselle left in charge of Christopher and Ruby—there was no choice but to depend on her—they drove the tractor to the calves' paddock.

Actually, Maggie drove the tractor. Blake stood on the footplate and hung on, feeling like a city kid, totally out of his depth.

He hadn't been on a tractor since he'd been six. He was riding as sidekick to save his cattle. He was Maggie's sidekick. He felt ludicrous.

Then he saw the calves and any temptation he had to laugh died right there.

They were in deathly trouble.

'The water's still rising,' Maggie whispered as she cut the engine. 'Oh, dear God, they'll drown.'

He stared out at the mass of water, at the terrified calves, at the impossibility of what lay before them. The calves could swim—most of them were swimming now—but they were all focussed on one thing and one thing only—the tiny island that was growing smaller while they watched.

'It's too late,' Maggie moaned. 'I thought I might be able to wade out there and drive them off. We could hack a hole in the fence higher up and you could guide them through. Once they see any of their mates on dry land they'll follow. But neither of us can swim out there and herd cows at the same time.'

They couldn't. Even if they were incredible swimmers, to swim and make cows follow directions would be impossible. Blackie was with them but a dog was useless as well.

There was a deathly silence while man, woman and dog watched the heifers struggle.

Then…

'The canoe,' Blake said, almost as an extension of his thoughts. All his focus was on the heifers. These calves were strong but how long until the first slipped under?

'Canoe?' Maggie's voice was a desolate whisper, but Blake's thoughts were firming.

'There's a two-man canoe under the house, or there was last time I was here. It's ancient. I've done some kayaking. I can handle it. But, Maggie, I can't do this alone. My stitches need protecting, plus I know zip about herding cows. But

I don't think I'll pull my stitches paddling. Not if I don't push myself.'

'What are you talking about?'

'I need to get the canoe up on the tractor. That'll require both of us lifting, but Liselle can help. We need to get it here and launched. Then… if we stick Blackie in the front, do you reckon you could persuade him to bark?'

'He'll bark on command.' And Maggie was with him.

'So we could get the canoe amongst them with a barking dog. If you told me what to do herding-wise…'

'Yes!' she said, and the desolation was gone. It was practically a shout. Maggie was suddenly a woman of action—a woman with a plan where there'd been no hope. She was already swinging herself back onto the tractor. 'What are we wait-ing for?'

It took them ten minutes to get back to the calves. Liselle had come out when they'd yelled and had helped heave the decrepit canoe out from under the house and get it up on top of the tractor in the driving rain. Somehow Maggie managed to drive with Blake holding the canoe steady—or as steady as possible, which wasn't very steady at all.

He had internal stitches, he thought ruefully.

If he had been his patient, he'd tell him he was out of his mind.

Eighty drowning calves didn't give him that option.

Maggie was gunning the tractor, not worrying about bumps, cutting corners, just going for it.

'Your other career's as a racing-car driver?' he demanded faintly, and she grinned.

'Eat your heart out. Oh, Blake, they're still there.'

She'd rounded the bend, the road disappeared under water and they could see them again, swimming in panicked circles around that tiny rise, fighting for a foothold.

In seconds the tractor was stopped. They shoved the canoe off—much easier getting it off than getting it on—then pushed it through the submerged road gate and into the water.

Maggie had brought bolt-cutters. As he climbed aboard and organised the paddle, she heaved the bolt-cutters in, lifted Blackie in as well, and slid in herself after that.

'Can you take me round the back?'

To the far side of the paddock? He could see why she needed to go there. The fence there was also under water but beyond the fence the land rose sharply. The dry land beyond was obvious, as it wasn't obvious where they were now. For the last couple of hundred yards they'd driven over a road a foot deep in water.

'I'll cut the fence there,' she said. 'I'll get them out if you and Blackie can scare them into swimming in my direction. They're terrified, but they'll follow a leader and they're not dumb like sheep. If you get the canoe near the island and shoo the calves there into the water they'll look for the next best option. Which will be me and a cut fence and dry land behind me. We can do this. Go.'

He went.

He'd had his appendix out a week ago.

She was under no illusions that this man should not be pushing a canoe through floodwater. He should be lying around in bed, convalescing.

She should never have asked him to help.

But the alternative had been to let eighty calves drown. She hadn't been able to do it, and neither could he.

Like he couldn't send away a baby?

He was soft in the middle, Maggie thought, but outside he looked as tough as the heavy-duty bolt-cutters she was holding.

He was wearing fawn chinos and a soft cotton shirt, with the top buttons undone and the sleeves rolled up to the elbows. He'd kicked off his shoes. The water was plastering his shirt to his body, delineating every muscle. His dark hair was soaked from the rain. Rivulets of water were running down his face but he wasn't brushing them away. He was totally focussed on what he was doing.

He looked like a warrior, she thought, suddenly and inappropriately. He looked lean and hard and dangerous.

She had a sudden flash of what this man would be like as a surgeon. She'd done a theatre stint in training; she'd watched men like this at work. They took lives into their hands…

She'd never been able to figure how they found the courage to take that first cut, but she could see it now. Surroundings were forgotten. Pain was forgotten—and he must be in pain—a week after an appendectomy it'd hurt even to laugh, and here he was, slicing the old-fashioned paddle through the water with total rhythm, total focus—as if he was paddling for the Olympics and not for cows.

'Blake…'

'Yes?' His response was clipped, hard, sharp, a surgeon in Theatre, wanting to know why a nurse was interrupting. He was focussed totally on what he was doing, but not so focussed that he forgot outside complications were possible.

She wanted to help. The stupid canoe only had one paddle. She could only sit like a princess, in the bow of the boat, holding Blackie.

'Steer well around the island,' she managed.

'I don't want them panicked further before I've cut the fence.'

'Fair enough.' The canoe's course altered slightly, and she thought that was no mean feat either. This canoe was ancient and high and wobbly. There were all sorts of obstacles in the water and the water itself was a mass of whirls and eddies. She was sitting as still as she could, as centred as she could, holding Blackie tightly as if by sheer concentration she could help this man.

He must work out. He must…she didn't know… run? He must do something to keep that lean body whip-sharp. His face was a study in concentration as he sliced across the current, and she could only guess how hard it must be.

She glanced across at the calves and saw one slip from the island, then get pushed under by another struggling to find purchase.

She held her breath but it surfaced again.

Eighty young cows, depending on one ailing surgeon.

Maggie, depending on one ailing surgeon.

Finally they reached the far fence. The water here was only eighteen inches deep. As soon as she could grab the fence wires, she was out of the boat, steadying her bolt-cutters.

'Stay,' she snapped at Blackie. 'Sit. Stay.'

He was a great dog. He whined but he stayed

in the bow as Blake turned the canoe and headed back out to the middle.

She hacked into the wires with a strength born of desperation then, as the last wire fell away, she headed out of the water, up the rise, so hopefully the calves could see the gap in the fencing, and see her standing on dry land beyond.

'Oi,' she yelled, trying to make the panicked calves look at her. 'Oi, Oi, Oi, Oi, Oi.'

Blake was behind the island now, cutting his way through the calves in the water, heading for the few on dry land.

'Speak,' she yelled to Blackie, and Blackie did just that.

He barked and barked, while Maggie yelled, and Blake manoeuvred his shaky little craft behind the herd, beached himself on the island, stood on the tiny piece of dry land and proceeded to remove the calves' last place of refuge.

He knew nothing about calves. They knew nothing about him, and maybe that was a good thing because they reacted to him and to the barking dog as if they were worse threats than the water.

The calves headed away from him, away from their target island. He was waving his arms like an idiot and Blackie was barking, so they launched themselves in the opposite direction—and suddenly they were swimming towards Maggie.

Maybe they knew her voice, or maybe she'd herded more cows than he had in his lifetime, but the calves seemed to be instinctively turning toward her.

If he was a calf, he'd turn toward Maggie.

There was a stupid thought.

He was hurting. He was standing on the only piece of dry land for fifty yards. He was waving and shouting like a fool—and he still had time to think… Think that Maggie was gorgeous?

She was wearing faded jeans and a shirt that had become almost transparent. She was soaked to the skin. Her chestnut curls were dripping around her shoulders, plastered to her face. Her feet were bare, she was yelling louder than he was…and the calves were heading toward her. And he knew why.

What was beautiful about her?

Bone structure? Facial features? Sense of fashion?

Um…none of those things, though the freckles and the gorgeous curves surely helped.

But it was the sheer courage of her. The way she tackled life head on.

The way she'd refused to care for his baby?

But she would care. He knew instinctively that she would. If he hadn't been here, if she hadn't figured he was more than capable of caring for his niece, then he knew she'd have taken her on, as she'd taken in Christopher last night, and Liselle, and he knew there only had to be a drama and she'd have more people sharing her tiny living space. That he'd offered to share his side of the house had seemed a blessing and a surprise to her. He wondered how many dramas she'd had since she'd moved into his tiny housekeeper's residence—but he knew without being told that without his urging, she'd never have let her life edge through the dividing door into his home.

Only it wasn't his home. It was a mausoleum of a homestead, redecorated in the fashion of the time by his mother and not touched since.

This morning, in bed, it had felt more like a home than it ever had in his childhood.

Because of Maggie?

'Oi!'

Her yelling had grown more insistent, riveting his attention totally on what was happening. The calves were shoving together in the water, seeking safety in numbers, swimming as a herd, but they weren't heading totally in the right direction.

They hadn't seen the gap in the fence.

Okay, boy, he thought grimly. Back in your boat.

'Are you okay?' Maggie called, and he thought all this and she was remembering his stitches.

'Blackie and I are fine,' he called. 'I'm bosun,

he's cox. If I can just persuade these calves to join us, we'll be a crew.'

His side was hurting. Badly. What had his surgeon said? No stretching for six weeks. Ha. Block it out, he told himself, and he headed for the calves, paddling hard, cutting through the water, focussing doggedly on what he was doing rather than the pain in his side. He was cutting the calves off from heading back to the island, herding them forward but sideways. He had to turn and turn again as the calves took fright and tried to scatter, but between them, yelling, barking, shoving the canoe at them, he and Blackie made them swerve and kept going.

They were exhausted, he thought, and he was expecting at any minute that one would slip under. They had to see…

The fence was about four feet high, so the gap was obvious. If they could see it they'd be safe.

'Oi,' Maggie yelled again, and Blackie barked, and he veered the canoe behind them—and the calf in the lead lifted its head as if casting round for one last desperate chance…

And saw.

And then the entire herd was surging through the gap. Maggie was stepping aside, the calves were through, rising out of the floodwater, finding their feet, scrambling onto dry land.

The calves bolted upwards as if the water was

chasing them. As they realised they were safe they turned into calves again. They looked like kids after a scary adventure, one they could boast about to their mates. A few kicked their heels like this was fun, yay, dry land, safe.

He was still paddling. He reached the gap and Maggie started pulling the canoe out of the water almost before he was out of it.

'I can...' he said, reaching down, but she slapped his hands away.

'You shouldn't.' And he saw she was weeping. 'I should never have let you. You'll have burst all sorts of internal stitches. I didn't realise until I saw you...how hard it was...that paddling was awful... I should never have let you do it and you'll have killed yourself and it's my fault.'

Okay, let's get rid of the drama, he decided. She'd been frightened enough for one day. He'd take himself out of the equation.

'I suspect I've killed my phone,' he admitted, hauling it out of his soaking back pocket and looking at it with apprehension. 'But otherwise I'm alive. And pretty damned pleased with myself.' Then, despite her objections, he helped her haul the canoe to dry land. What harm would another pull be when there'd been so many?

But she still looked terrified. She still looked... like the sky was about to fall.

He tried not to notice. He looked at the calves,

turning into kids again. Then, because he couldn't help himself, he looked again at this bedraggled slip of a woman, standing with the rain mingling with her tears, and he felt something change inside him...

Something he'd never felt before.

She was gorgeous, he thought. She was simply, unutterably, indescribably gorgeous.

She'd put everything she knew into saving these calves, and now she was feeling guilty. Guilty for saving calves that weren't even hers. Guilty for risking hurting him. Guilty even for his damaged phone?

She was unbelievable.

And before he knew what he intended, before he even realised what he was doing, he'd tugged her into his arms and held her close.

She'd been terrified, and in truth he'd been the same. Out of his comfort zone. Hurting. Worried the dratted calves would drown.

It wouldn't hurt to hold her, to comfort her— and to take comfort in return.

But...was this about comfort?

He held her close, closer, and he felt the thump of her heartbeat against his, and thought maybe it wasn't.

'Yay for us,' she whispered, and her voice was muffled by his chest. 'You were great. Are you sure you're not hurt?

'I'm not hurt,' he said, and then as her heart kept on thumping, he thought it had been terror for him as well as terror for the calves that was making her heart race.

He cupped her chin with his hand and tilted her face so he could force her to look at him. Her eyes were huge. Her eyes still held remorse and fear.

'I'm fine,' he said. 'I'm great and you're terrific.'

And then, as she kept gazing up at him, he couldn't resist.

He kissed her.

One minute she was feeling like she was losing eighty calves and ripping Blake's stitches to bits and there wasn't a thing she could do about it.

The next she was being kissed so thoroughly, so amazingly that there wasn't a thing she could do about that either.

Not that she wanted to.

If she wished, she could pull away. He wasn't holding her so tightly, so strongly that she couldn't tug back and get him to release her.

But how could she tug back when she was being kissed…like this.

Fire meeting fire.

Fire?

How could she be feeling heat, when she was cold and dripping and shaking from reaction to what had just happened? There was no answer and even as she asked the question, she forgot it.

She forgot everything.

There was only the feel of this man's mouth. The fire, the heat, the strength and warmth and… the maleness of him.

There'd been too few men in Maggie's life. Too little opportunity. Too little time.

This was hardly an opportunity, hardly the time, but there was no way she was pulling back.

Her lips opened, seemingly of their own accord, welcoming him, wanting him.

Wanting him?

Yes. She did want him. Her body seemed to mould itself to him all by itself. Her breasts crushed against him, their wet shirts disappeared almost to nothing, so nothing seemed between them but white-hot want.

His mouth was exploring hers. His hands were in the small of her back, tugging her closer, and hers did the same to him. She was melting into him, dissolving, aching to be closer, closer, closer…

She'd never felt like this. She'd never dreamed she could feel like this. Her entire body was on fire, every sense screaming that here was her man, she was part of him, she belonged.

Maybe it was supposed to be a kiss of relief and of comfort. It was surely a kiss of need—both of them needed the assurance of human contact, that they were safe and life went on and they'd suc-ceeded—but it was more than that.

It was a kiss that changed her. It was a kiss that made her feel as she'd never felt—as if every sense was suddenly alive.

Sleeping Beauty, wakened by a kiss?

Well, that was ridiculous.

There was a tiny part of her mind that was still analysing. It was like she was falling off a cliff and thinking as she fell, How am I feeling right now?

She was feeling pretty good, actually. No mat-ter about the ground rushing up, she was feeling pretty amazing.

Where had this heat come from? What was making her feel like her entire body was sizzling, waking from slumber and turning into something she didn't know it was possible to be?

She was falling and she didn't care.

So far it was so wonderful.

How high was the cliff? How long could she stay in freefall, savouring this moment, the feel of him, the strength, the way his hands held her, the way she seemed totally enfolded, protected, frail even…

Strong Maggie, melting at a man's touch.

Strong Maggie, melting and loving it.

And then Blackie barked.

He'd done his bit. He was expecting praise. Expecting attention. Or maybe it was that his mistress was being mauled by a strange man and the dog was confused and wondering what he should do about it.

He barked again, and finally, achingly, Maggie tugged away.

Freefall over, she'd reached her destination. She almost expected to feel shattered. That was crazy but she did feel… Bruised? Dazed? Exposed?

Confused was the least of it.

'Well, that was unexpected,' Blake murmured, and something in his deep, growly voice said he was almost as confused as she was. 'Adrenalin, do you think?'

'Either that or it's something in the water,' she managed, and carefully turned away and looked up the hill.

The calves were settling. They were high up on the hill, and as they watched, a couple put their heads down and started to graze.

Back to life as they knew it.

Right, she told herself, trying not to feel breathless. Trying to make this strange, needy… *kissed*?…sensation go away. Trying to go back to life as she knew it. 'That's that fixed. Well done, us. And thanks, Blake, I could never have done it without you.'

'They're my cattle.'

'They haven't been your responsibility for a very long time.'

'Maggie?' He hadn't turned to watch the cows. He'd stayed watching her the whole time—which wasn't doing anything for the state of her discombobulation.

'Mmm?'

'They're my responsibility, and thank you,' he said. 'And thank you for the kiss. It was…'

'Nice,' she said hurriedly, before he could say anything more. 'It was very nice indeed, but there's no need for you to be worrying that I expect to take it further. We might be staying in the same house but there's a door with a lock between us.'

'And two kids and a baby.'

'That, too.' She hesitated. 'I don't know what came over me.'

'Over *us*.'

'Over us,' she repeated, though she wasn't sure where me and us separated in the kissing stakes. 'But…' She tried hard to get her feet on firm ground—a bit hard when she was standing in six inches of water. 'I…I have work to do. Are you sure you're okay? Can I check your scar?'

'No!'

'I didn't think so,' she said, and she managed a chuckle. 'But you would tell me if there was something wrong, wouldn't you?'

'Probably not.'

'That's reassuring.'

'I hurt,' he told her. 'But there's no piercing pain. I think I've pulled but not torn. Bruised but not broken. Should we take this canoe back over the far side and see if we can get it back up on the car?'

'Let's not,' she said faintly. 'For eighty calves I was prepared to let you risk it. Now I'm thinking of your stitches again. We'll secure it here in case it's needed again but that's it. I'll walk the long way round and bring the tractor home. You head over the rise and reach the house without getting even more wet.'

'Maggie…'

'Mmm?'

He stared down at her. She was adjusting the canoe, tying the rope to a fencepost.

She was suggesting—no, decreeing—they go their separate ways.

That was surely sensible. That's what this woman was. Sensible.

She was also vulnerable—and beautiful.

She was also saddled with kids and family and responsibility, chained to a life that was alien to everything he knew.

Maggie waded back to the tractor, skirting the worst of the high water.

The road was only a few inches underwater. They could never have headed the calves this way—to push them forward when all they could see was water would have been impossible—but the road was still safe enough to drive on.

She'd still be able to get back and forth to her clinic, she thought, which was just as well.

She'd be needed.

The locals had never thought the dam could burst. She made a fast mental list of the houses close to the river and thought none would be so close to water level that they'd be flooded. The early settlers had been wary of floods and had built accordingly. There'd have been more than just Maggie and Blake desperately trying to move stock in a hurry, though. People would be doing stupid things, putting themselves at risk.

As Blake had put himself at risk.

She should never have asked it of him. The man was a week out from an appendectomy, and for him to manoeuvre the canoe as he had…

He could sue her, she thought grimly, but then she thought, They were his calves. He could have said let them drown.

He couldn't—as he couldn't evacuate Ruby and hand her over to others.

Her thoughts were running off at crazy tangents. She was thinking of the way he held Ruby—of the way he looked at her. There were things going on in Blake's background she had no idea of. He looked at Ruby and he almost looked…hungry.

She grinned at that, thinking, Nope, big bad wolf wasn't the image she was going for.

So, hungry for what?

What sort of childhood had this man had? His mother had been glamorous and flighty—the local gossip was that she'd married for money. His father had been an oaf. Where had that left him?

And why had he kissed her?

She put her fingers to her lips as she walked, thinking they felt…different.

Why had he kissed her?

'Well, who wants to know?' She said it out loud and kicked a spray of water up in front of her. 'You? You know already. We thought the calves would drown, we got them out, and in moments of triumph, people kiss.'

Only it hadn't been like that. At least, it hadn't been like that for her.

'And that's because you're close to a thirty-year-old spinster without a life of your own,' she snapped, and kicked up more water. 'That's because every minute of every day is taken up with your work or your family, and your hormones are telling you it's not enough.

'So what are you intending to do about it?'

She laughed at that, morosely, because some

questions already had answers. Some questions weren't even worth asking.

What was she intending?

One big fat nothing.

She had a job. Almost half her pay went towards helping the kids out with what they needed so they'd get the qualifications she had, tickets out of the valley, escape paths from the cloying demands of her mother. Apart from one tiny, tiny nest egg, the rest of her money went on living. Putting one foot in front of another. Doing her job and keeping the kids safe.

In a couple of weeks the water would be down and Blake would be gone. End of story.

But maybe, while he's here…

'Don't even think about it,' she told the silence, and she kicked so hard the water went up and over her, making her wetter than ever. 'He's my landlord and if he hasn't burst anything today he's a doctor who can help if I need him. Nothing more. Put yourself back in your box, Maggie, and stay there. Now.'

CHAPTER SEVEN

HE got back to the homestead—and there were more kids.

Plus Maggie's mother.

Liselle was on the veranda, clutching a sleeping Ruby, and looking almost as if she was holding her mother at bay.

'Dr Samford,' Liselle breathed when she saw him, and there was real relief in her voice. 'I…I didn't invite her.'

Then Maggie arrived. She pulled in through the gate, climbed from the tractor, squelched across and joined him—and looked at her mother.

'Mum,' she said blankly, and Barbie beamed. She was standing by an ancient family wagon. She hauled up the tailgate and lifted out a suitcase.

'This is lovely,' she said. 'I was so pleased Dr Samford's decided to share. Did you remember our living-room roof is leaking? I told you last week, Maggie, and you've done nothing about it. And now the dam's burst and the kids are scared.'

She was dressed as a hippy. Fiftyish, long, flowing skirt, beads everywhere, vivid dyed-blonde hair hanging past her shoulders.

Shudder territory.

And obviously Maggie thought so, too.

'You're not staying here,' she said, in a cold, dead voice that had Blake glancing at her sharply. She sounded like she was in pain.

'Well, I'm not staying in that house by myself.' Her mother's voice became shrill and accusing. 'You can't expect me to. I had to sleep in Susie's bed last night because there was a drip right by mine, and both the kids are whining for you.'

Susie verified the statement by sidling across to Maggie and tucking her hand in her big sister's.

Blake saw Maggie's shoulders slump.

She looked like a deer caught in headlights, he thought. She'd escaped her family, but her family had tracked her down.

'Can you carry my suitcase inside, Dr Samford?' Barbie said—and simpered.

It was her right to be looked after.

Blake looked at her and looked at Maggie. Barbie was a world away from the woman who'd been his own mother but there were similarities. He was sure she'd married his father for money and she'd gone on to marry three other men who were expected to look after her every whim. Right now she was in the States with yet another besotted lover.

Maggie's mother had never had the beauty or the style to attract lovers to obey her commands but the way she was looking at Maggie now, he knew the story. Maggie had been the servant. Maggie still was the servant.

No more. A line had to be drawn, and Maggie's face had him drawing it.

'Maggie's brothers and sisters are welcome to stay until the waters recede,' he said. 'But no one else. The evacuation notice says that if anyone's worried, they can camp in the local hall. If the kids want to join you there, that's fine.'

'You're not separating me from my kids!'

'Of course I'm not.' Blake strode up the veranda steps and lifted Ruby from a stunned Liselle's arms. 'I'm not fussed if your kids stay here or not,' he said, in a bored voice that told her to take it or leave it. 'If Maggie wants them to, then that's fine. If you don't permit it, then that's fine, too. All I'm saying is that the invitation is for kids only. Sort it out between you. I need to feed Ruby.'

And he walked in the front door—on his side of the house—and closed the door behind him, leaving all the Tildens on the other side.

Maggie came to find him ten minutes later. He was in his kitchen, fixing formula. He had Ruby nestled in her drawer-cum-bed by the fire stove. He was feeling incredibly domestic.

He was also feeling like he'd been sucked into another world. Babies and kids and dogs and cows and mothers.

And Maggie.

She opened the kitchen door and it was all he could do not to drop the bottle he was holding and take her into his arms. He'd never seen a woman look so…caged.

'I'm so sorry,' she managed. 'But they all want to stay. I can't make them go with her.'

'She's not staying.' He made his voice flat, definite, sure. He spooned formula into the bottles and when he glanced at her again a little of the tension had eased.

'She thinks you mean it. She's not game to call your bluff.'

'It's no bluff. She walks in, I'll pick her up and throw her out.'

'Can…can I ask why?'

'Because she makes you cringe,' he said. 'That's good enough for me. I don't know what's gone on in your past, Maggie, but I know appalling parenting when I see it. I avoided my father and I continue to avoid my mother. You should be allowed to do the same. Has she gone?'

'Yes, but all the kids are here.'

'The whole eight?'

She managed a smile at that. 'No. Just four.'

'Then it's five, counting Ruby. We have ourselves a houseful.'

'Blake, I didn't mean to impose—'

'If you had meant to impose—like your mother certainly meant to impose—I would have sent you packing as well,' he told her, still concentrating on his bottles. Surgical precision was required. Ruby wasn't going to get anything but perfect milk on his watch. 'I extended the invitation, Maggie, not you,' he added. 'I can see the kids are scared and they need you. They're welcome to stay here, but only until the road is open again. This isn't open-ended.'

'You're fantastic.'

'I'm not,' he said shortly.

'Yes, you are,' she said, and her eyes misted. 'Heroic. Like you told Chris he was. But you've done more. You've saved him, you've saved your cows and now...you've taken in my whole family.'

'But you don't want them here.' It was a question, a guess—and it found its mark.

She stilled. She watched him, then watched her feet and took her time answering.

'I have this dumb dream,' she said at last. 'From the time I first remember, it's always been: "Maggie, watch your brother. Take Liselle for a walk. Stay home from school today because your father and I have a gig..." It's just...how it is. Mostly I accept it, only every now and then I dream that I'm backpacking round Europe, sipping kir in a café on the Left Bank in Paris, or watching the sunset over the Nile and having no one talk to me for hours on end.

'It's a dumb dream but it stays. When the kids are older, that's what I decided I'll do. Then recently—when Mum and Dad split—I realised they're getting dependent as well. I'm starting to be scared that after looking after their kids all my life I might end up looking after them.'

'It's not going to happen.'

'No,' she said softly. 'That's why I moved out. Blind terror, if you like. But the kids still need me. I'll probably end up going home.' She took a deep breath. 'But not tonight. Tonight you solved my problem for now. You let me care for the kids and you've forced Mum to be independent—and it didn't even have to be me who was nasty to do it. Plus you saved all those heifers. To watch them drown would have killed me. I should never have asked you but I couldn't bear not to. But now...'

She glanced down at Ruby, who was wide awake but not complaining yet. There was time. 'Now I'm checking your tummy,' she decreed. She motioned to the leather-covered bench at the side of the huge kitchen. 'Sit. Lie. I want to see.'

'There's no need.' To say he was astonished was an understatement. She'd been grateful and emotional, but suddenly she was brisk again, efficient—and bossy. 'I'm fine.'

'For me,' she said, still implacable. 'If you think I can calmly sleep tonight knowing you might have done yourself damage...'

'Maggie...'

'You're a hero,' she said, and she grinned at him. 'Heroes are brave enough to bare a little skin.'

'I'll check myself.'

'Doctor, heal thyself?' she quoted. 'I don't think so. Humour me. Lie down.'

'Maggie...'

'Just do it.'

He gazed down at her and she gazed back—implacable, immoveable, strong as iron. This woman had raised eight children, he thought, and right now he felt like a ninth.

'Now,' she said, and lifted the bottle from his hand and set it on the bench. 'Do it.'

Why not?

Because he felt vaguely foolish? Because he felt exposed; vulnerable? Because he didn't want this woman thinking of him as a patient?

All of which were dumb reasons.

He was sore. He had pulled his stitches.

Sensible was the way to go—surely.

He sighed—and went and lay on the bench and tugged his shirt up and undid his belt.

If this was Miriam he wouldn't mind, he thought. Their relationship could be professional—it usually was. So what was different about Maggie?

He had no answer. He could only lie and wait and submit.

He had hurt himself. She'd seen him wince as he'd climbed from the boat. She'd also seen a tell-tale spattering of blood on his pants and she'd known she'd have to check. He also knew it was sensible, she thought. The guy in him didn't want her near him. The doctor in him said submit.

He submitted. He hauled his shirt up, undid his belt, and she unzipped his pants before he could protest.

His abdomen was rock hard, muscled, ripped. As his shirt fell open she was hit once more with the sight of a male body that was pure muscle. She felt the strength of him as her fingers touched his skin while undoing his zip.

She glanced up at him and saw his face set hard. She wasn't hurting him. She was barely touching him.

This man didn't like being exposed, she thought. This was a guy who walked alone.

But not tonight, she thought ruefully. Five children, two dogs, and her. She was taking over this guy's life.

She wouldn't mind…

Um, no. For the sensation of that kiss had flooded back, and suddenly Maggie Tilden wasn't feeling professional at all. She was bending over a near-naked man—which she'd done before, she was a nurse, for heaven's sake—but she wasn't feeling like a nurse. She wanted…

She could want all she liked. She couldn't have—*and this man was a patient.*

Focus.

She focussed.

He had torn the wound open, just a little, right at the top. The internal stitches must still be holding, she thought, examining the wound with care, as there was no sign of swelling, no sign of internal bleeding. And Blake might look uncomfortable but he wasn't writhing in pain.

There was only an inch or so that had pulled apart a little and bled, and even that wasn't terrible.

'It's okay,' she told him, glancing up at him and seeing him with his hands behind his head, staring straight at the ceiling with a look so grim he might as well be expecting her to attack with a scalpel. 'Hey, I'm not about to dive in and have a fish around,' she joked. 'I thought I might settle for a wash, some disinfectant, some steri-strips and orders for a good sleep.'

His face lost a little of its severity but, she thought, he was forcing himself to relax. He was well out of his comfort zone.

'Want to tell me what's going through that head of yours?' she asked, expecting him not to answer, or to deflect the question, but to her surprise he did answer.

'The last time I lay on this couch, it was because my father hit me,' he said. 'I must have been about five. He spilt my face above the eye. Minor stuff. My mother put a plaster on and screeched at him the whole time. Funny thing, though. No matter how much he hit me—and he did—it took the knowledge that he'd been sleeping around before she took me away.'

'Then I guess you have Ruby—or Ruby's grandmother—to thank that she finally did take you,' she said, forcing her voice to be light. She was carefully cleaning, focussing on the wound, not the man—but part of her was thinking this man had been incredibly isolated. She was so surrounded. Which was worse?

Blake's childhood, she thought. Her parents were dodgy as parents went, but they'd never hit, and the tribe of nine kids had provided their own love and support to each other.

She dared another glance at his grim face and thought, Absolutely, crowds every time.

She'd crammed his house with kids and dogs. She was doing him a favour, she decided—and she grinned.

'What's funny?'

'I'm just thinking of the great protective screen I've erected round you,' she said. 'Five kids and me and the dogs... No one can hit you now, Blake Samford.' She dried his skin with care and thought that no one could hit him anyway. Not with those muscles. But she wasn't telling him that. There was no way she was admitting—even to herself—how awesome she found his body. She started adjusting steri-strips, gently tugging together the slight gaps where the wound had parted. Her concentration was absolute.

He didn't speak, just lay and stared at the ceiling, but the rigidity had gone. She'd defused the moment, she thought. Kids had to be good for something.

'I'll dress it...'

'I don't need a...'

'Remind me to ask next time I need medical advice,' she said severely. 'You'll be dressed whether you want it or not.'

'Very civilised,' he said, and she chuckled, and dressed her carefully applied steri-strips and then went to tug up his zip.

His hand closed over hers.

'I can do that, at least,' he said, and his hand held…for just a moment too long.

He needed to sit up. Instead of tugging her hand away, she gripped his and tugged—and he rose a little too fast.

She was a little too close.

A lot too close.

They'd been here before. She'd kissed this man. This man had kissed her.

He was so close. He was so…so…

Compelling? For he'd placed his fingers under her chin and was tilting…

'No.' Somehow she managed to say it. Somehow she hauled some vestige of common sense from the back of her addled brain and made herself step back.

Her foot hit the bowl of water on the floor, it spilled and she was almost glad.

'Look what you made me do,' she said, a trifle too breathlessly. A lot too breathlessly.

'If you'd let me kiss you, you wouldn't have tripped.'

'You don't want to kiss me.'

'And you know that because…?'

'Because I come with encumbrances.' She stalked over to the pantry—she'd spent six months nursing Blake's father so she knew her way around this place—and grabbed a wad of old dishcloths. She tossed them onto the floor, then went down on her knees and started drying. 'I'm a workhorse,' she said, scrubbing with more ferocity than she needed to. 'Not a show pony. You're only kissing me because I'm the only female available.' She sat back on her haunches and glared. 'But you're wrong. You have Ruby who has need of all the kisses you can give her. Concentrate on what's important, Blake Samford.'

'I'm thinking you're important, Maggie Tilden.'

'Then think again,' she snapped. 'You're trapped, you're wounded, you're exhausted, and I have the right chromosomes. Nothing more. Get a grip.' She pushed herself to her feet, which was hard when she realised he'd stepped toward her to help and she had no intention of letting him help. She gathered the bowl, the dressing wrappers, the dishcloths and turned away.

'This is the main house,' she muttered. 'I live in the servants' quarters. My brothers and sisters might have infiltrated their way over here but me...me, I'm scared stupid. Leave it, Blake. I have a flood, a dependent community and a dependent family, and I need no other complications. None. Your wound is fixed. You need to feed Ruby and put yourself to bed. By yourself,' she added, as she saw what looked suspiciously like laughter in his dark eyes.

'You're overreacting.'

'That's the story of my life,' she muttered,

stalking to the door. 'Setting boundaries and hoping people respect them. And being told I'm overreacting when they don't.'

'Maggie…'

'I have to check I'm not needed at the clinic. Liselle will look after my kids.' She glanced down at Ruby. 'You look after yours. Goodnight, Blake.'

And she walked out and closed the door behind her.

What had just happened?

Blake stared at the closed door and thought he'd just been hit over the head with a sledgehammer. That's what it felt like.

He'd really, really wanted to kiss her. The need had felt extraordinary, but it hadn't been a simple sexual urge. It had been all about the smattering of freckles on her nose. The shadows under her eyes. The way she'd stood in the top paddock and yelled, 'Oi, oi, oi.'

It had been about the way her fingers had felt, gently touching his skin. She was a nurse. She'd been doing her job but it hadn't felt like that. It had felt…electric. It was as if everywhere she'd touched there had been this frisson, this connection, two halves desperate to come together.

But it wasn't true. His half was all for it. Her half was backing away like a startled rabbit.

Did she think he was about to seduce her? Local landowner taking advantage?

His father's reputation had gone before him.

She didn't know him.

And he didn't know her, he told himself. She was like no one he'd ever met. There was no artifice about her—what you saw was what you got. She was taking care of this valley, taking care of her siblings, taking care of…him?

At his feet Ruby finally tired of waiting. She'd been perfectly patient while her uncle had been treated, but enough was enough.

She opened her mouth and she wailed.

Maggie wasn't taking care of Ruby. Fair enough, he thought ruefully. He could hardly expect it of her.

As if in rebuttal, her head appeared around the door.

'You should be in bed,' she said, and she sounded reluctant, like this was her conscience talking. 'If you like, I'll feed her and we'll take care of her on our side for the night. Only for tonight, mind.'

'You're going back to the clinic.'

'There are five of us. One thing the Tilden kids learned early is to take care of each other. For tonight only, we can do it.'

She would, too, he thought. She was looking at

him and seeing a guy who was recovering from appendicitis, who'd pushed himself too far.

He did not want to be this woman's patient.

'Ruby and I will be fine,' he said, a bit too shortly.

'You're sure?'

'I'm sure.'

'Knock if you change your mind,' she told him, sounding relieved. 'And I'll check when I get home. Sleep tight, Blake. Sleep tight, Ruby.'

She closed the door again—and he felt even more...

Like he wanted the door to stay open.

He fed Ruby.

He wandered out to see what the kids were doing.

Ruby had gone to the clinic. The rest of the kids were in his big sitting room.

Liselle was hunched over a side table with a bunch of books in front of her that looked truly impressive.

'Calculus?' he asked, checking over her shoulder.

'Yes,' she said tersely.

'Trouble?'

'This,' she said, and pointed hopelessly. He sat and helped her integrate a complex equation, with techniques he thought he'd long forgotten, and felt absurdly pleased with himself when it worked.

If Maggie was out saving the world, he could at least do maths.

Susie was under the table with her dolls.

Christopher was propped up on cushions, his leg high in front of him. The painkillers would be making him feel sleepy but he'd obviously decided he wanted to be with his siblings. He was watching something violent on television. Was it suitable for a twelve-year-old? But then he thought these kids must be pretty much independent by now.

'It's okay,' Liselle said briefly, seeing him watching the TV and reading his doubt. 'Maggie and Chris go through the guide once a week, Chris reads out the reviews of what he wants to watch and they negotiate.'

Fair enough, he thought, feeling awed.

He looked down at Ruby, who was still in his arms, and wondered who'd negotiate for her.

What was this baby doing to his head? He'd had one image of his baby sister, embedded in his memory thirty years ago. He'd hardly thought of her since, and yet this little one, a baby of that baby, was calling to something he hadn't been aware he had.

A need for family?

He gazed round the living room, at the kids sprawled over the furniture. Sleepy Christopher with his bandaged leg, who'd come so close to death but was recovering fast. Susie, spilling out from under the table with her dolls. Pete with his video games and Liselle keeping vague watch as she studied. Maggie must have lit the fire before she'd left—or maybe Liselle had. They were independent kids, but he just knew...

Threaten one and you threatened them all.

Family.

Ruby was dozing in his arms. He should put her to bed. He should put himself to bed, he thought. He didn't understand the way he was feeling...

It was all about weakness, he decided. It was the after-effects of appendicitis, the shock of Ruby's arrival, working with Christopher and the physical demands of rescuing the calves.

And the way he was feeling about Maggie?

Um...no. Family. Maggie. That was emotional stuff, feelings he'd long suppressed because they ought to be suppressed. He had a very practical, very satisfactory life and the sooner he could go back to it, the better.

'You look tired,' Liselle said. 'You want me to cuddle Ruby until Maggie comes home?'

So Maggie could come home and see that he hadn't managed one baby?

'Thank you,' he said gravely. 'But I'm fine.'

'Call us if you need us,' Pete said, emerging from his computer game for a moment. 'I've buried nappies before,' he offered nobly. 'One spade, one hole and the job's done.'

The kids chuckled and so did he, and then he escaped.

They were great kids, he thought, and then he thought of Maggie.

They weren't great kids because of their parents, he thought. They were great kids because they had a great big sister. An awesome big sister.

A really cute, really sexy, big sister.

That was exactly what he didn't want to think. He needed to think of practicalities. Ruby. Bed.

Not Maggie.

She had two patients to see at the clinic. Both minor complaints. Aida Batton had cricked her neck lifting piglets out of a sty that was becoming waterlogged. Anyone else would have figured that driving the sow out first and leaving the piglets to follow was the best option, but Aida considered herself an earth mother, and thought the sow might slip in the mud and squash one of her babies—and now she was paying the price.

Maggie gave her a gentle massage, sent her home with anti-inflammatories and a heat pack, and was promised a side of bacon in exchange.

Robbie Neal—a mate of Christopher's—had decided to use the run-off from the hill beside his house as a water slide. He'd used a tyre tube, there hadn't been a lot of control from the beginning and he'd hit a tree. He had grazes and bruises everywhere but as far as Maggie could see, the damage was superficial.

No hint of loss of consciousness. No sign of head injury. She cleaned him up and sent him home with his long-suffering parents.

She cleaned the clinic, walked through into the hall where the locals had set up a temporary evacuation centre, noted that her mother wasn't there—she'd be sponging on any of half a dozen neighbours, she thought grimly, no communal evacuation centre for Barbie—and then she thought she shouldn't care.

How did you turn off caring?

She drove home thinking just that. And also… how did you stop yourself starting to care?

For a guy who'd kissed her?

It was nothing, she told herself fiercely, but unbidden her fingers wandered to her lips as if she could still feel…

'I can feel nothing,' she said harshly into the silence. 'I can't afford to feel anything. Honestly, how many complications do you want in your life? A womanising Samford is exactly what you don't need.'

A womanising Samford…

She was tarring him with the same brush as his father, she thought. Was that fair?

Of course it wasn't. Up until now he'd been awesome. He'd helped her care for her little brother. He'd saved his life. He'd saved his cows. He'd dispatched her mother.

He'd kissed her.

'Which has turned you into a simpering school-girl,' she snapped. 'Grow up, Maggie. It was only a kiss.'

Only it didn't feel like just a kiss. It felt…so much more.

The house was silent. It was eleven o'clock and she was dead tired.

She checked the fire, checked each of the kids, made sure Christopher was okay.

Christopher and Liselle both stirred and hugged her as she leaned over them—something they'd done since they'd been babies.

Part of her loved it.

How could she ever walk away?

She couldn't, she thought, as she tucked them in and kissed them goodnight. When Blake sold the farm she'd move back home. Of course she would. The events of the day had shown her just how dangerous it was to leave the kids with her mother.

Tonight she didn't even have the luxury of her own bed. Susie had demurred at sleeping in a big, strange bedroom by herself. She was very definitely sharing with Maggie.

It's fine, Maggie told herself. You've had six months' luxury of having your own place. That's it.

She was so tired…

But she did need to check on Blake. Just in case, she told herself. He'd pushed himself past the limit this afternoon. If he was bleeding internally, if he was in pain, would he call her?

Maybe he wouldn't and the nurse in her wouldn't let herself go to bed without checking.

She slipped through the darkened house. His bedroom door was open, just a crack.

She had no wish to wake him—or Ruby—if he was asleep. She pushed the door just enough for her to slip inside.

He had the curtains wide open. The clouds had cleared for once, and the almost full moon was lighting the bed, the man sleeping in it, and the baby tucked in her bed beside him.

They were both soundly asleep.

Blake was bare to the waist. He was sleeping right on the edge of the bed, and his arm was trailing down so his fingers were resting beside Ruby's face.

It was as if he'd gone to sleep touching her.

Giving her human contact. Letting her know he cared?

Something was twisting…

This man…

Don't, she told herself fiercely. No. Put your hormones right back where they belong.

He stirred and she backed out of there so fast she almost tripped over her feet. He was fine. She didn't need to check again.

She didn't need to go near this man when he was half-dressed, or in his bedroom, or when he was smiling, or when he was feeding Ruby, or when he was doing any of the stupid, dumb things that were mounting up that made her feel…

Like she had no business feeling. When the river went down he'd head back to his city hospital, to his independent life, and she'd just…

Just…

She needed to get a grip. Any minute now she'd be putting something violinish and maudlin on the sound system and start weeping into her beer.

The phone rang and she grabbed it with real relief. Work. That way lay sanity—not looking at half-naked men in the moonlight.

But the phone call wasn't for her.

One problem with sharing Blake's house was that she shared his phone.

Bob Samford's existing line had never been disconnected. An extension of that same line rang in her apartment. She'd been covering the costs since she moved in.

Maggie had a cellphone. The locals knew it, but they disliked using the longer phone number and contacting her cellphone was a more costly call.

When she'd lived with her mother, no matter how much she'd discouraged it, they'd rung her there. As soon as she'd moved, they'd simply phoned here. So when the phone rang as she reached the hall, she answered it fast, to stop it waking the house.

'Maggie Tilden,' she said, polite and professional.

'Who is this?' a female voice demanded.

Uh-oh. She didn't recognise this voice. It was cool, slightly arrogant and startled. Like she was expecting someone else.

She guessed this was Blake's call.

'I'm the district nurse,' she said, a tad too quickly. 'Maggie Tilden.'

'The woman living at the back of Blake's house?'

How could you dislike a woman after two sentences? Not possible. She got a grip and managed a bright smile. Someone had said smile on the phone and the person at the other end could hear it. She tried—hard.

'That's right,' she said, determinedly chirpy. 'Did you wish to speak to Blake?'

'Yes.'

'I'm sorry, but he's asleep.'

'It's only eleven.'

'Yes, but he's had a very big day. He had to save his calves from drowning and Ruby needs feeding in the night.' She paused. 'I'd rather not wake him.'

'He's not answering his cellphone.'

'He dropped it in the water. I don't believe it's working.'

There was a deathly silence. Then, 'He's been in floodwater?'

'I… Yes.'

'To save calves?' It was practically a screech.

'Yes.' She was trying to be polite—but this was hurting her ear.

'You won't look after the baby—*and you expect him to save cows?*'

'They're his cows,' she said mildly. 'And it's his baby.'

'It's not his baby.'

'He's taking responsibility for her.'

'He has no right—'

'It's his sister's baby,' she said gently. 'He has more right than most.'

'You're the midwife. He says you won't—'

'Be professional? I'm being exceedingly professional. I don't take patients home.' She glanced behind her and winced at the mess the kids had made of Blake's fabulous, faded living room— and thought actually she'd brought everything else home.

'Blake needs help,' she snapped. 'He's ill. If you're a nurse, help him.'

'I'm doing what I can.' She'd coped with belligerent patients before—and their relatives. She was deliberately keeping her voice calm, unruffled— but implacable. 'I don't believe there's any need to worry. I'd prefer not to wake him, though. If you give me your name, I'll tell him you called.'

'Miriam Donnington,' she snapped. 'Dr Donnington. Blake's fiancée.'

Why did her stomach lurch? No reason at all.

Or lots of reasons. How stupid did she feel? How had her hormones led her down a path she didn't know she was treading until right now?

Blake belonged in another life. He was a city doctor with a city fiancée. He was trapped here. The kiss they'd shared had been the result of adrenalin, from shared danger and from victory and nothing more. She'd known it. She just… knew it better now.

So why was she standing silent, she demanded of herself, as if she was in shock? Get over it, she told herself harshly—and sensible Maggie emerged, as sensible Maggie always did.

'I didn't know he was engaged,' she managed, and somehow she kept her smile firmly in place. 'Congratulations. I can see why you're concerned. I'll let him know you've called. I suspect his phone might still be out of action even when it's dried, but you can usually raise him on this number. Unless he's asleep. I'm trying my best to keep him in bed.' She listened to how that sounded and decided maybe she'd better lighten it. Make it even more professional. 'He's not a very co-operative patient,' she confessed, nurse to doctor.

'Blake knows what's good for him,' Miriam snapped. 'He doesn't need a nurse telling him what to do. What he needs is peace, not a nurse and a baby complicating his life.'

'Plus my four kids,' she said, letting her temper emerge just a little, deciding why not tell it like it is? Even wind it up a little.

He'd kissed her. He had a fiancée. Toe rag!

'Four kids?'

'Blake doesn't mind,' she said cheerfully. 'All my kids are here. Pete says Blake's even been playing his computer games with him. Now, was there anything else you wanted?'

'I… No.' She sounded stunned.

'Goodnight, then,' Maggie chirped, still managing to smile, and she put the phone down—and turned to find Blake watching.

* * *

He was leaning against the wall, arms crossed, bare chested, bare legged, ruffled from sleep—simply watching.

He destroyed her professional detachment, just like that.

Nurse, midwife…woman? With Blake around she was all woman, and her body reacted accordingly.

Fiancée. Fiancée.

Keep your head. Get off that dratted path.

'Miriam?' he asked, and she nodded.

'Your fiancée.'

'That's what she told you?'

'She wanted me to wake you. I refused. I'm sorry. You can ring her back.'

'I will.' His eyes searched her face. 'She gave you a hard time?'

'For not looking after you—which might be justified. If you were being flown out right now with internal bleeding, I'd be to blame.' She was sounding so calm she was proud of herself.

'As you said,' he said mildly, 'they're my cows. My choice. And, yes, Maggie, Ruby's my niece.'

'Will Miriam help you take care of her?' It was none of her business, she thought. She shouldn't ask, but the question was out there now, like it or not.

'Someone has to,' he said. 'Unless I take Pete's way out and bury the nappies.'

She managed a half-hearted smile back at him. 'Pete'd bury dishes, too, if it was up to him. But good luck. You should ring her back. She sounds genuinely worried.'

'I will. And, Maggie…'

'Mmm?' He was too close, she thought. Too close, too big, too bare.

'I'm sorry she upset you.'

'She didn't.' How was that for a lie? 'I'm accustomed to my patients' worried relatives.'

'I'm not a patient,' he said, so softly that she shivered.

'You ought to be,' she managed. 'It'd be a whole lot easier if you were.'

And before he could retort she'd turned and headed into her own small apartment, closing the door very firmly behind her.

He should ring Miriam right back. Instead, Blake stood and watched the closed door for a very long time.

Maggie was behind that door.

She'd be in bed with her ten-year-old sister. His father's two dogs would be under her bed. She was surrounded.

Miriam would be at her desk in their cool, grey and white apartment with a view of the harbour.

His fiancée?

She wasn't. Why had she said it?

To protect him, maybe? To stop Maggie thinking she could take advantage?

Was she taking advantage?

No. Ruby would be here even if Maggie wasn't—and he'd invited her siblings to stay. As well as that, he'd talked to the doctors who'd cared for his father. Without Maggie the old man would have been hospitalised far earlier. Bob had been no one's idea of an easy man but Maggie had worked to make his last months as good as they could be.

She was not a woman to take advantage…

Fiancée…

He rang and Miriam answered on the first ring. 'Blake…I knew you'd be awake. That woman wouldn't fetch you.'

That woman. It sounded…wrong.

That woman was Maggie.

'She's doing a hell of a job,' he said mildly. 'She's taking care of the whole valley.'

'Not you. Were you really dumb enough to stand in floodwater?'

'If I hadn't, eighty calves would have drowned.'

'For heaven's sake, Blake, what's worth more? All that skill, all that training…'

'Not to mention me,' he said mildly. 'Even without the medical degree I'd still have missed me.'

'For heaven's sake,' she snapped.

And he thought…he thought…

Fiancée?

They'd drifted into this relationship. They'd competed against each other at university, studied together, pushed each other. They were both driven.

He wondered suddenly whether, if he didn't have his medicine, would he have Miriam?

Would she want him?

Would he want her?

It was a crazy thing to think at midnight, when his feet were cold on the floorboards and he could hear Ruby starting to stir in the background, but think it he did.

'When the water comes down,' he said, speaking slowly, thinking it through as he spoke, 'I'd like you to visit here before I come back. I'd like you to get to know Ruby. Help me make a decision about her.'

There was a sharp intake of breath.

'What sort of decision?'

'She's my family, Mim.'

'I'm not Mim.' Suddenly her voice was almost shrill. 'I'm not taking on anyone else's baby. I don't even know if I want one of my own yet.'

'Of our own?' he queried.

'I… Yes.'

'Fiancée?'

There was a moment's pause. It turned out longer. It ended up stretching a very long time indeed.

'I said it for your benefit,' she said at last. 'I thought you might need it. If you're staying in the same house...'

'We have five kids staying here now,' he said gently. 'They're chaperons enough. But...are you thinking I'd need them?'

'I don't care what you do,' she said fretfully.

There was another silence at that. 'Really?' he said at last, and he looked at the closed door and thought of Maggie in bed with Susie and the dogs underneath and he thought...Maggie was a woman who cared.

'Look, this is a dumb conversation,' Miriam snapped at last, regrouping. 'What we have is sensible, Blake. Do you want to mess it up?'

'Would it mess it up if I was unfaithful?'

'If I were to know about it, yes.'

'And if you didn't?'

'Look, I don't care,' she snapped. 'I'm tired and I have a long day tomorrow and if you want to have a torrid little affair with your tenant/nurse— *who has how many children*?—then it's fine by me. But there's no way I'm coming down there.'

'No,' he said bleakly, and he glanced behind him, to his open bedroom door, where he could see Ruby's bedclothes wriggling. Any minute now she'd open her mouth and yell.

And then, suddenly, he was thinking of Maggie again, and Christopher, and his television rules. Boundaries. And he thought…if ever he had an affair with Maggie she'd give him boundaries—and they wouldn't be do what you like but don't tell me about it.

'I'll be moving apartments when I get back to Sydney,' he said, and he heard Miriam's breath draw in with shock and with anger.

'So it's true. Your stupid little nurse…'

'It has nothing to do with Maggie,' he told her, though maybe it did, and it was simply too soon to acknowledge it. 'But it has to do with family. You and me, Mim…we're friends. Colleagues. But we've never been family and it's too late to start now. Our relationship needs to stop. It's going nowhere and it's time we acknowledged it. I'm sorry, Mim…Miriam, but it's over.'

'So you're starting…what, a family? Down there?' The viciousness in her voice was appalling.

'I have no idea where or what I'm starting,' he told her. 'All I know is that we're wrong. Thank you for trying to protect me, Miriam, but I don't need a fiancée. I'm not sure what I need. Oh, actually, yes, I am. I need to make one bottle for one baby and then go back to bed. Right now, I'm not capable of thinking further.'

CHAPTER EIGHT

THE river stayed impassable. The rain was interminable. There was nothing for it but for the valley to hunker down and wait.

If anyone had told Blake he could spend a week trapped in a farmhouse with five children and be…almost content, he'd have labelled them crazy, but that's exactly what he did.

Maggie was frantically busy. That rush of water through the valley had caught everyone unprepared. There'd been stock loss—nothing dire, but farmers had been caught by surprise and there were sprains and bruises from rushing to save stock, grazes that had turned septic from floodwater, leg abscesses that had got wet and stayed wet too long, back problems as people heaved belongings higher than the water.

Blake helped when he could, relishing the times he could go out with her to the outlying farms, helping to debride ulcers, double-checking her diagnoses, or just plain giving reassurance that

Maggie was right, they didn't need evacuation to the hospital over the river.

To his surprise, he was enjoying it. He'd never thought of country medicine, but its variation was almost…fun.

But frustrating for Maggie.

'What is it about having doctor in front of your name?' she demanded. She'd spent an hour telling Maisie Goodall her leg was starting to heal and the antibiotics were taking effect, but Maisie was still frightened. Blake had walked in, examined the ulcerated leg for a whole two minutes and smiled his reassurance.

'This is healing beautifully, Miss Goodall. See the faint film over the edges? That's slowly working its way in to form a seal. Try and keep it elevated and dry, watch lots of telly, cuddle your cats—' the woman was surrounded by them '—and I reckon by the time the water's down you'll be good as new.'

Maisie almost purred as loudly as her cats, and Maggie climbed back into her car beside Blake and glowered.

'I can speak until I'm blue in the face,' she muttered. 'But you walk in with your doctor-ish bedside manner and you don't do a single thing and suddenly Maisie doesn't want a helicopter, she just wants another visit from you tomorrow.'

'Basic Bedside Manner,' Blake said smugly.

'Taught in med school. Kept secret from nurses for generations.'

'You mean you're good looking, you're male and you smile at her,' she snapped.

'There is that.' He looked smug and she had to chuckle.

'Okay, it's useful,' she conceded. 'If I could just bottle you and keep you in my medical kit...'

'I won't be put.'

'No.' She sighed. 'You shouldn't even be out here.' She'd brought him out of desperation because Maisie had been so scared, but she kept reminding herself that he, too, was a patient. But he was recovering. He was moving with ease, the stiffness and the grimacing had gone and he was well on the way to recovery.

They had Ruby in the baby seat. Bringing her with them for the minor stuff meant Liselle could keep studying and, besides, patients liked it. Maggie had no doubt there'd be a pair of bootees from Maisie's knitting needles by the end of the week. That was okay as well because it meant Maisie would sit with her leg up while she knitted. That'd help her healing—but healing was what Maggie should be organising for Blake, rather than letting him accompany her on her rounds.

But he seemed to enjoy it, she conceded, and he was very skilled, very efficient, very friendly— and very useful. Also accepted. Because of his links to the valley the locals treated him as one of them. Local boy made good.

Also local boy made interesting—and there was the complication. Interest meant speculation. The locals looked at Blake, they looked at Maggie, they looked at Ruby—and Maggie could see exactly what the valley was thinking. That made her think...and thinking was exactly what she was trying not to do. It was bad enough having Blake sitting beside her, but a girl didn't need to think about it.

She glowered at the steering-wheel—and the ignition light lit up.

Excellent—a diversion.

Or maybe not excellent. Ignition light...trouble?

She should be driving a Health Services car on her rounds. Normally she would, but the bridge closure had happened earlier than expected, catching them all by surprise. Her dependable hospital car was on the other side of the river and she was left with her own.

Which wasn't so dependable. She used it in emergencies, but patients had been known to groan when she pulled up in her battered wagon.

Ignition light...

'What's wrong?' Blake asked as she pulled over to the verge.

'Sister, farmer, nurse, mechanic,' she said. 'You've met three. Welcome to the fourth.'

She climbed out and hauled up the bonnet, and he climbed out after her.

Cars weren't his thing. Yeah, he could drive them, but his garage was right by the hospital and apart from the odd tyre change he'd never concerned himself with them.

Underneath the bonnet looked as decrepit as the outside of the car, and a lot more mysterious, but Maggie was sighing and heading for the rear.

'Panty hose,' she said.

'Panty hose?'

'A girl's best friend. Never go anywhere without them.' She hauled out a pair of black tights that looked like they'd seen better days. 'Can you find some scissors in my bag and chop the legs off?' she asked. He did, while Maggie did…other stuff.

'Fanbelt?' he guessed, thinking he ought to try and sound intelligent. They were in the middle of nowhere. Where was the nearest tow truck?

But Maggie wasn't thinking about tow trucks. 'You've got it.' She was head down in the engine, tossing out a very decrepit belt. 'I did a course a while back to learn what to do. The fanbelt transmits drive from the engine to the alternator and water pump. Without it, the battery doesn't charge and the engine overheats. It's okay. I have a spare at home and the panty hose will get us there. I just need to make a smooth knot so it'll spin. I'll loosen the alternator mounting bolts and push the alternator towards the other pulleys. Then I'll slip on my pantyhose, lever the alternator until the loop's tight and do up the bolts. I'll only use the crank and pump pulleys. It's hard to make the panty hose tight when it's fitted over more.'

'Right,' he said faintly, and she glanced back up at him and grinned.

'So mechanic doesn't fit in your job description.'

'No.'

'Lucky you.' She straightened and took the chopped panty-hose leg from him. She had a smudge of grease on her nose. He thought she looked…she looked…

'Hop back in the car,' she said gently. 'I can cope on my own. Miriam would have my hide if she could see me dragging you with me on my medical rounds—and I don't need you to hold my spanner.'

'Miriam's not my fiancée,' he said, and she paused and stared at him—and then bit her lip and dived under the bonnet again.

'Not?'

'She's a colleague.'

'She said—'

'She's been my partner. Sort of. We studied together at university. When we got jobs at the same hospital, we figured we could afford an amazing apartment if we got it together.' He hesitated. 'That doesn't totally sum up our relationship,' he said honestly. It's drifted past friendship but the other night...I realised it needs to stop drifting.'

'Because I was sharing a house with you?' she said, not looking at him, concentrating fiercely on whatever it was she was concentrating on. 'Because you kissed me? If you think I'm taking responsibility for breaking up your relationship...'

'I didn't say that.'

'You want me to phone her and tell her there's an oak door and five kids between us?'

'I already have.'

'Then it's ridiculous.'

'Is it?'

'Of course it's ridiculous.' She thumped something with a spanner. 'You've lost a potential fiancée. Why aren't you sounding heartbroken?'

'Because I'm not in love with Miriam. Neither of us has ever pretended to be in love with the other. Because, even though I've known you for less than two weeks, even though it makes no sense at all, the kiss we shared was electric and I've never felt that with Miriam. Ever. So moving on from Miriam...it had to be done. It's not fair on anyone to continue.'

There was a moment's silence. Deathly silence. Actually, it was more than a moment. It lasted for a very long time.

Then the spanner thumped again. She went back to work. He waited—and he thought…

Why had he said that? Confessed all?

Because her backside under the bonnet was really, really sexy? Because the smudge of grease on her nose made him want to wipe it away for her and then kiss it? Because the whole package of Maggie, woman, sister, farmer, nurse, mechanic was doing something to him he couldn't understand and he couldn't fight?

She was the most desirable woman he'd ever met.

He'd suggested what they had together was unique. One kiss?

He'd done this all wrong. He'd confessed he'd been blown away by a kiss, while the woman in question was covered in grease and doing something a guy would traditionally do but which he had no hope of doing.

Had he scared her?

He *had* scared her. He saw it in her body language. He saw it in the way she concentrated fiercely on doing what she had to do.

He'd been really, really stupid.

Why?

He thought up a barrage of excuses. Appendix. Floods. Baby. Maggie herself.

The kiss.

Together they were a package designed to

knock any man off kilter, he decided—and maybe Maggie realised it. When she finally hauled herself back from under the bonnet she had her face under control.

She dropped the bonnet into position with a bang, wiped her hands on the remains of the panty hose, slid into the driver's seat and waited until Blake had climbed back into the car beside her.

She started the car, watched the ignition go out with satisfaction, pulled back onto the road and finally, eventually she spoke.

'I hope what you said back there was an aberration,' she said.

'It was…a fairly awesome kiss,' he said, thinking caution was the way to go here.

'Fairly?'

'Okay, very,' he conceded. 'And just now… There was grease on your nose. You looked sexy as hell. I love a girl with a spanner.'

She managed a smile at that, but it was a wobbly smile.

'Just as well I've put my spanner away, then,' she said. 'Blake…' Her voice turned serious. 'Don't read anything into what happened between us, and for heaven's sake don't call things off with Miriam because of me. I come with a lot more encumbrances than a spanner, and I'm not in the market for a relationship. One kiss does not a relationship make.'

Where could he fit caution into this reply? He tried, but failed. When in doubt, opt for honesty. 'One kiss makes me feel like I've never felt before,' he said, and it felt okay. It felt right.

'It was a good kiss,' she conceded. 'But don't even think of taking it further. I'm heading for Africa.'

'Africa?' he said, startled.

'And possibly Siberia. Not to mention Sardinia, Istanbul and Paris. All by myself. I have a bank account…' She took a deep breath, glanced at him—quickly—and obviously decided to go on. 'When I was a kid I used to collect drink cans,' she told him. 'Outside footy matches, from the richer kids at school, wherever I could find them. I squashed them and sold them by weight. They made me a pittance but it was *my* pittance. When things got bad at home I used to escape and search for cans. Even today I think of escape in the form of drink cans.'

She hesitated then, and he wondered why she was telling him this—why she was turning what must surely be a joking conversation—a mistake?—into a conversation about saving. But something in her expression told him this was important. And maybe it was something she'd told no one else.

'Mum and Dad were always broke,' she told him. 'Desperately broke. If they'd known I had even a tiny fund they'd have used it in an instant and it'd be gone, so I kept hiding it and they never knew. All my life I hid it. As a teenager I babysat, like Liselle does. Some of the money I earned went into my secret fund. When I started nursing I kept doing it, squirrelling away my pittances. Ninety-nine per cent of all I've ever earned has gone to keeping me or helping the kids, but one per cent is mine. My tiny fund is almost enough to get me to Africa—but not back.'

'But you will come back?' he asked, startled, and she shrugged and grinned.

'Of course I will. I suspect the family will always need me—Good Old Maggie. But I will go.' It was a declaration, almost a vow. 'The moment Susie leaves home, I'm off.'

'Susie's ten,' he said faintly. 'That's seven years.'

'I'll have the return fare by then,' she said resolutely. 'More. The less they need me the more I'll be able to save. I'm aiming to travel for at least six months. All by myself… Remember that backpacking dream I told you about? Sitting on the Left Bank in Paris drinking kir, with not one single person to answer to. Lying in the sun on a Greek island. Seeing a rhinoceros in the wild. I really do hope to turn that into a reality one of these days.' She glanced across at him and bit her lip and turned her attention deliberately to the road again. 'So don't you—and Ruby—dare mess with my dream!'

'I wouldn't dare.'

'Good,' she said. 'Just so we understand each other.'

They drove on and he kept right on kicking himself. Of all the morons… Why had he frightened her? Why had he made a big deal out of one kiss? Why had he forced her to tell him her life dreams?

He'd known this woman for little more than a week. He'd kissed her once. To suggest it could be the foundation of a relationship…to tell her it was the reason he'd broken up with Miriam…

The whole thing was dumb.

He was a city surgeon, ambitious, career focussed, totally centred on getting as good at his job as it was possible to get. Maggie lived in Hicksville, surrounded by kids and cows and not even the scent of decent coffee.

And never the twain should meet.

It was cabin fever, he told himself. He'd been trapped with Maggie for a week now. Any more time in this place and anyone with an X chromosome would start looking good. Even a woman with grease spots on her nose.

Only it was more than that, he conceded as they drove on. Maybe Maggie represented something he'd never thought about—or maybe something he'd repressed. A need for home?

He'd lived in this place until the age of six. After that, his mother had moved from place to place, from man to man. This valley must have some sort of long-term emotional hold over him.

And then there was Ruby. He glanced behind at his tiny niece, sleeping deeply in her baby cocoon.

What to do with Ruby?

She needed family, and right now she had it. She had him, and Maggie as back-up, and she had four siblings, Liselle, Pete, Chris and Susie, who all regarded her as their personal plaything.

She was starting to smile and everyone in the house was working for those smiles.

'Hey, I got one. I'm in front by two.' That had been Chris that morning, crowing with delight, and the memory made him smile.

The way Maggie handled Ruby made him smile, too. While he was unwieldy when Ruby was distressed, Maggie stepped in, calm and sure, and made things right.

But even put together, those things weren't enough to define as love. To start thinking long-term relationship...

Nostalgia. Need. Isolation.

A girl with a grease spot on her nose.

Weakness and need was all it was, he told himself harshly, but now he had Maggie looking at him like he had a kangaroo loose in the top paddock. She'd even felt the need to explain her long-term life plans, spelling out that they didn't include him.

Which was all fine—only why was he sitting here thinking he'd made a huge mistake? It was because something within him was telling him Maggie was important for far more than practical or nostalgic reasons. Maggie was someone the likes of whom he'd never met before and might never meet again.

Maggie. Grease spots. Maggie. Love and laughter.

Yes, she came with terrifying baggage—but to have the right to hold her…

He'd known her a little more than a week and he'd scared her.

'Cabin fever must be getting to me,' he said into the loaded silence, and she cast him a glance that contained…gratitude? He was letting her off the hook. Setting things back to normal?

'It must be,' she said, sounding relieved. 'You should ring Miriam and tell her isolation's playing with your head.'

'Can isolation happen in a house with five kids, two dogs and how many cows?'

'It comes in all forms,' she said, and her voice changed a little, and suddenly he heard a note of desolation. 'I've been surrounded all my life and

I've longed for isolation, yet in a sense I already have it. Define isolation?' She took a deep breath. 'Sorry. It's getting to me, too. You're right, cabin fever. We need to avoid kissing—we're likely to jump each other through sheer frustration. But the authorities are saying the water level's starting to drop, and the forecast is for the weather to finally clear. Within a week they'll set up a barge. The kids can go back to school. You can go back to Sydney. Life can get back to normal.'

'Is that what you want?'

'Of course it is,' she said tightly. 'I have a seven-year plan, remember? I've been working on it since I was ten years old and I have no intention of deviating from it now.'

But she was deviating.

Only in her mind, she thought savagely. Only when she let herself turn from practical Maggie into someone who let her mind wander all along sorts of crazy, impractical paths.

Paths that ended with Blake.

She should avoid him. She couldn't.

They went home and it was time to redo Ruby's legs. She'd been wearing casts for a week now. They needed to be removed, the tiny feet manipulated some more, inched closer to normal, and new casts applied.

So Maggie watched and helped as Blake tended his tiny niece with all the care in the world.

At least she could focus on Ruby rather than her uncle.

Left unattended, these feet would cripple this little girl—they'd make her life a torturous nightmare, with a wheelchair a real, long-term option.

But once the casts came off she could see improvement. The feet had been twisted far back at birth. They were still twisted, and left now they'd revert, but at rest, the little feet lay at an angle that was slightly closer to normal.

'Can you run her a bath?' Blake asked, as he started playing with the tiny feet, and she did. Well, okay, not a baby bath—this place didn't run to it—but the kitchen sink was big, porcelain, perfect. She did a quick scrub, filled it with warm water and lined it with towels so Ruby wouldn't be lowered against the hard surface.

She half expected Blake to hand Ruby to her, but it was he who lowered her into the water. It was Blake who looked down as Ruby's eyes widened with surprise at this strange, new sensation.

They'd bathed her the night she'd come, before the first cast had gone on, but she'd been a very different baby then—malnourished, abandoned, unloved.

This was a Ruby who'd had a full week of regular feeds, regular cuddles—a regular family?

It wasn't exactly regular, Maggie thought, thinking of her weird assortment of brothers and sisters handing her around—but now Ruby had the thing she most needed in the world. A constant.

Blake.

He was holding her as if she was the most precious thing in the world. She hardly needed to have put the towels down—his hands held her with warmth, security and love.

Love?

She looked into his face and saw emotions she didn't understand.

This man was falling for this baby, she thought, and he was falling hard.

Blake Samford was a city doctor, aloof, a stranger. He was nothing to do with this valley or her. He'd sell this farm and be gone from her life.

But today he'd said...

Forget what he'd said. Concentrate on Ruby, not Blake.

But some things were just plain impossible. The way he was looking at this baby was twisting her heartstrings. This was no doctor looking at a patient. Neither was it a man who planned on handing Ruby to foster-parents as soon as he could.

He was an enigma, and even though she'd sworn to stay distant, she couldn't help herself. She wanted to know more.

'Tell me about your sister,' she said, as Ruby discovered she could wiggle her arms and her cast-free feet and feel even more amazing sensations in the warm water. 'About Wendy.'

'I never knew her.'

'I think you must have,' she said gently. 'The way you're looking at Ruby.'

And then, amazingly, he told her. He cradled Ruby and played with her while he talked of a baby he'd seen only once—a baby who'd destroyed his parents' marriage.

He told of being six years old and crouching by the baby while everyone around them yelled. He told her of placing his hand in the baby's carry-cot and feeling her finger tightening around his. He told of being six years old and terrified and thinking this baby was his little sister and she must be terrified, too.

And then he talked of the strange woman taking her away, of his parents never speaking of her again, and of his family no longer existing.

'A psychologist would have a field day,' he said, half mocking.

And she looked up at him and thought…and thought…if he hadn't been holding his baby she'd touch him. She'd run her fingers down that strong cheekbone and caress the lines of pain and self-mockery.

The image of tall, dark, dangerous was receding.

There were worse things than being one of nine neglected kids, she decided. This man had been alone all his life.

But now he'd found Ruby.

Focus back on Ruby, she thought desperately. That was the plan. She had to have a plan around this man because she did not want to feel like she was feeling. It seemed like a vortex, a whirlpool, dark, sweet, infinitely enticing, but who knew what lay inside?

'Don't you need to manipulate?' she managed, and he glanced at her and caught himself and she saw him swap—with difficulty—back to professional as well.

'Of course I do,' he said. 'And it might be easier if we do the first part while she's happy in the water.'

So he handed her over, and as their hands touched as they inevitably had to during handover, and she held his baby while his big, skilled hands manipulated those tiny legs with all the tenderness in the world, as she stood close to him and watched his face and watched his hands, she realised she was in so much trouble.

He'd broken off a relationship with Miriam because of one kiss. That was crazy.

But maybe the condition was catching.

Warm, dry, fed—and confined in her new cast— Ruby was fretful. She'd had a lovely time when her whole body had been free to move, and now she was back to being constricted. It'd be a long haul, Blake thought. Six weeks of casts, an operation to cut the Achilles tendon to let it heal in the new correct position, months of twenty-three hours a day in a brace, then more in a brace at night.

'It's the price you'll pay for being able to dance at your wedding,' he told her, but she wasn't taking any comfort from that.

She was tired after her bath, and so was he. His mate back in Sydney had been right—the operation had knocked the stuffing out of him. Maggie didn't need him right now. He could settle on his bed with Ruby beside him, and try and settle her.

Tell her stories of what their life would be like together?

For he was keeping her—as simple as that. Some time during the last week she'd twisted her way around his heart and she was staying.

He'd be joining the ranks of single dads.

How did they cope?

How would he cope?

How would he cope without Maggie?

'Is that what the conversation in the car was all about?' he demanded of Ruby. 'Or is it my subconscious knowing it'd be easy if she fell for me—if she took you on as well as her brood.

After all, she's stuck here for the next seven years anyway.'

There's a romantic way of looking at a relationship, he thought wryly. Red roses didn't even begin to cut it in comparison.

But it had to be more than that. The way he was feeling…

'How can I know what I'm feeling' he asked Ruby, and watched her eyelids grow heavier and heavier until she drifted off to sleep. 'Yeah, I'm smitten with you, and that's cracking open places I don't want to go. I want my independence.'

How could he be independent and keep Ruby?

Make Maggie fall in love with him? Work out how to bend his career so he could fit in family? Live happily ever after.

Was that independence? There was a part of him that was saying it was a solution to all their problems—but another part of him was telling him he'd be giving up way too much. Even if Maggie agreed.

But Ruby was so needy, and that kiss… The possibilities were there. As he watched his tiny niece sleep and thought of Maggie next door, with the weight of the world on her shoulders, he decided a man had to try.

The forecast was saying it would be another week before the river would be safe to cross. He wasn't due back at work for another two weeks.

Anything was possible in two weeks, he thought. Including making a family?

He'd never thought about a family. Why was he thinking about one now?

She had enough of a family without including him. She told herself that over and over during the next few days, and she meant it.

As much as possible Maggie kept her brood on her side of the oak door. They had to use Blake's large sitting room—there wasn't enough room for them anywhere else—but the kids were under threat of death not to disturb him. She cooked for her siblings and fed them in her own small kitchen. The kids thought they should invite Blake, too, but it seemed…dangerous? Inviting him into her tiny kitchen or letting her brood loose in his seemed equally fraught.

She needed to stay apart. That kiss…telling her he'd split with Miriam… It was a sweet seduction, she told herself fiercely. He'd get her over to his side of the house, she'd fall for Ruby and she'd be trapped again. Man gets landed with abandoned baby, man makes moves on motherly nurse… Coincidence? Ha.

So she needed to be firm. Doing his own cooking was part of caring for Ruby, living with her, making a life for her. It was part of Blake's bonding process that was proceeding beautifully. She wanted no part in it, and she wasn't interfering with it for the world.

Occasionally she needed him medically. Occasionally he needed her for advice on Ruby. That's all the contact they needed, she told herself, and anything else was scary.

But the kids kept on telling her she was nuts. Even cruel.

'When you're not here he comes in and plays computer games with us, and helps me with maths, and he even helped Susie tie hair ribbons on her doll,' Liselle told her. 'We love playing with Ruby. Only when you come in and he's here, you back out again so he doesn't come in when you're home. That seems mean.'

It did, Maggie conceded. But it also seemed safe. She was being defensive, and somehow she had need of all the defences she could muster.

'And he makes life less boring,' Pete muttered from the couch. 'I'm so-o-o bored. The guys are making mud slides on the far side of the valley. Tom's taking them over in his dad's car. If Tom's dad says it's okay, why won't you?'

Because Tom's father was a moron and Tom behind the wheel was a danger to everyone, Maggie thought, but she didn't say so.

'You know Mum's forbidden it,' she said, more mildly, because she'd worked on this one. Barbie didn't particularly care what her kids did, but Maggie had learned that if she put her under enough pressure—like threatening to withdraw financial help—Barbie could be persuaded to utter edicts. *'You won't drive with Tom.'*

Pete couldn't tell his mates Maggie said no. 'Mum says no' hurt his pride less.

'Mum doesn't care,' Pete said sullenly. 'Tom says she's staying at Archie Harm's place. She hasn't even phoned to find out how Chris is.'

'She does care,' Maggie said, without conviction. 'And you're not to go with Tom.'

'Then let me ask Blake to play this video game with me. It's too hard for Chris, and Liselle won't.'

'Don't disturb Blake.'

'Why not?'

'Because he's not part of our family,' Maggie snapped. 'He's our landlord. Nothing else.'

The week dragged.

The longer the river remained impassable the busier Maggie became. Medical niggles became major. The authorities organised helicopter drops of essentials and evacuation of a few people who'd just got sick of staying.

Maggie's mother was one of them.

'Archie and I are fed up,' she told Maggie on her first phone contact since Chris had hurt his leg. 'You have the kids. Why should I stay? We're visiting Archie's daughter in Sydney.'

'Can you take Pete?' Maggie asked, knowing already what the answer would be but she had to try. 'He's so bored I'm scared he'll do something dumb.'

'You think Archie's daughter wants kids?' Barbie asked incredulously. 'Of course she doesn't. Pete's a good boy. You worry too much, Maggie.'

And she was gone.

Maggie had been using the phone in the hall. She turned and found Blake watching.

Sharing the phone had to stop, she thought. Why wouldn't her mother use the cellphone? Why was Blake watching? And why was her mother's voice so shrill that she knew Blake must have heard?

'Archie?' he asked.

'He's a no-good dropkick from the other side of the valley,' she told him, trying to keep her tone unemotional. 'His wife keeps leaving and then he hangs round Mum. It doesn't last. They'll have a fight, his wife'll take him back and things will get back to normal. As normal as they ever do in our family.'

'So you're totally trapped.'

'The river's trapping me.'

'Even if it goes down…'

'I'm fine,' she said. 'I just need to stay close.'

'When I sell this house, where will you go?'

He saw the colour fade from her face. How

many places were available for cheap rent in the farming district close enough to be on call for her siblings? None.

She'd go back home.

'Maggie…'

'It's my business,' she said. 'You have enough on your plate worrying about Ruby.'

'Maybe we could—'

'Maybe we couldn't,' she snapped. 'Maybe there's no we.'

She walked back into side of the house and carefully closed the door behind her. That was rude, she thought. Uncivil. She didn't even know what he'd been about to say.

But there was something about the way he'd looked at her.

There's no *we*.

It was true, she thought. No matter how he looked at her, it was simply another tug at her heartstrings. She had too many already. A guy with his needy baby…

A guy as drop-dead gorgeous as Blake?

A guy who'd hand her yet another responsibility?

'Maggie…' It was Chris, yelling from the other side of the door, Blake's side. 'Pete's got the remote and won't give it to me. Tell him he has to.'

'Pete,' Blake's voice boomed. 'Give your brother the remote or I'll switch the channel to the National Bowling Championships and burn the remote. I mean it.'

There was a loaded silence and then a chuckle and then silence reigned from the living room.

She smiled.

She told herself not to smile.

Because that smile was all about thinking *we*.

There was only manipulation and responsibility and she'd had enough of that to last a lifetime.

CHAPTER NINE

The household grew more and more tense. Maggie was doing her best to keep the kids happy and not bother Blake, but the valley needed her. She was out a lot.

The weather stayed appalling. Half the problems she was called out for were as the result of people having too much time on their hands—and too much imagination.

'Maggie, I've found a lump on my back. I think it's cancer.'

'Maggie, I've got this funny rash on my neck and I've been reading on the internet about Scabies...'

'Maggie, you know that scary cow disease? Jacob something? My mum used to make me eat brains when I was a kid, and how do I know I don't have it?'

If the river's staying up, the valley should be cut off from the internet, she thought bitterly. The internet was the greatest hypochondria feeder of all time, and she was stuck with it.

Luckily she had Blake. He was great at hosing down panic. By the end of the second week they'd worked out a system. She'd take the initial call. If it was minor and practical she'd go. If it was hysterical and sounding like it could be solved by talking, Blake would go—usually with Ruby, as Ruby herself distracted and defused fear.

If it was major they'd both go, but so far there'd been only a couple of real dramas. A local farmer had rolled his tractor onto his leg. Blake had been calm, steady and impressive, and she'd been truly grateful for his presence. Amy Southwell had had a major heart attack. There had been nothing either of them could do there, but Maggie had watched Blake comfort Amy's husband of sixty years, grip his shoulders, simply hold him.

She'd thought again—quite desperately—there was no *we*. How could it ever work? A city surgeon with baby and a country nurse with eight siblings.

So stay separate, she told herself, and she did, mostly, until Pete got too bored to continue to obey, climbed into a car with a kid who shouldn't have a licence—and nearly got himself killed.

Maggie was dressing an ulcer on Rose Chibnell's leg when her phone went. It was Tom's mother.

Cindy Blayne was a fluffy piece of silliness, and she and her husband let their son do exactly what he wanted. Tom was eighteen going on twelve, and Maggie hated Pete being friends with him.

'Maggie?'

Cindy's first word had Maggie's catching her breath. She could hear terror.

'What's wrong?' She stepped back into Rose's hall, knowing whatever was coming was bad.

'Maggie, Tom's rolled the car.'

A car accident. It was the worst of nightmares in such an isolated place. Her mind was switching straight into triage. She'd need Blake, she thought, and then she remembered he wasn't home. He'd headed over the ridge to see the Misses Ford, who'd decided they both had jaundice, going on for liver cancer. Thanks to the internet.

His cellphone was still out of action.

She'd ring the Ford house. She had to find him.

'Where's the crash?' she asked. 'Where's Tom?'

'Maggie, it's not Tom who's hurt.' Cindy sounded like a trembling mess.

'What do you mean, it's not Tom?' But her heart did this strange, cold clench. Already she sensed what was coming.

'He picked up Pete from your house,' Cindy quavered. 'I know your mum said no, but she's been away and Tom and Pete thought... Anyway, they were in the car together and Tom's okay but

Pete was thrown out and he's down the river bank and Tom can't reach him.'

'Dr Blake?'

Miss Harriet Ford answered the phone and handed it to Blake with all the solemnity of a well-paid secretary. Blake took it and another elderly lady was on the other end.

'Dr Blake, this is Rose Chibnell,' the lady said, primly but urgently. 'Maggie's asked me to try and contact you. There's been a motorcar accident at the junction where the river turns north and the road twists away from it. It's Tom Blayne's car.'

He already knew who Tom Blayne was. It was amazing how many of the valley people he was getting to know.

'Is he hurt?'

'That's why Maggie needs you,' Rose said. 'She doesn't know. At least, she knows Tom's okay, but it seems her brother, Pete, was in the car with him. He was thrown out and Tom can't reach him. Tom thought he heard him groaning but he's too far down the river bank for him to see. Do you want me to call the medivac helicopter? I can ask for it to be put on standby.'

'Yes,' he snapped. 'Please. Now.'

And then he turned and looked at two astonished spinsters who didn't have jaundice, much less liver cancer.

'How are you at babysitting?' he demanded, and handed over Ruby before they could reply. 'Thank you,' he said, and went.

Tom was slumped on the roadside, by the steepest incline down to the river in the valley, and Maggie could see at a glance what had happened.

The edge of the road was sodden. Tom had come round the bend too fast and hit the verge. The verge had started to crumble, he'd swerved, overcorrected, hit the bank with the far side of the car, flipped it and rolled.

He was very lucky the car hadn't gone right over.

Maggie wasn't thinking luck, though. She was thinking…Pete.

She was out of the car, bending over Tom, shaking his shoulder. His eyes looked glazed. Shocked. He wasn't a bad kid. Just stupid.

He was bleeding from a cut above his eye but it was shallow, bleeding sluggishly. It was enough to look dramatic but not enough to distract her from her urgent questioning.

'Tom, are you hurt? Apart from your eye?'

'N-no.' He was staring downwards with horror. She glanced down and her heart lurched.

This was no small landslip. The road had given

a little, but a little had become a lot as it had slipped downwards. She saw a swathe of fresh, tumbled mud.

'Pete…'

'There's no seat belt on the passenger side,' he muttered. 'It broke last month. Dad was s'posed to fix it. Pete fell out.'

'Pete's down there?' She'd forgotten to breathe. She'd forgotten everything.

'I can't get down. I tried and the mud moves. I heard him groan at the start but not any more. I can't… You reckon he's dead?'

Dear God.

She stared again at the mud. She cupped her hands and yelled, louder than she'd ever yelled before.

'Pete!'

No answer—but the river was roaring beneath them.

Oh, God, how far had he slipped? How much mud was there? Where…?

Tom was weeping, wringing his hands. She grabbed his shoulders and forced him to look at her.

'I need your help,' she said. 'You know the local numbers. Ring Mrs Mayes, or if you can't get her ring Ted Barnes or Fred Halliday. Tell them I want the emergency chopper with paramedics,

and I want tractors and I want as many men as
you can get, as fast as they can possibly get them
here. And I want them to find Dr Samford. Do
you have that, Tom?'

'I… Yes.'

'Ring, fast. Ring everybody. I'm going down.'

'You can't.'

'I'll go down at the edge of the slide,' she snapped.
'I don't have a choice. Phone, now.'

Clambering down a sodden cliff face beside a
mass of tumbled mud and debris was easier said
than done. It was appallingly difficult.

She had no choice.

She called as she climbed but she felt…hope-
less.

There was too much mud. If Pete had been
thrown as the mud had slid he could be buried.
He could have been pushed into the river.

She was weeping and climbing and yelling—
and the bank was too steep. The rocks were giving under her feet.

Slow down, she told herself. You're no use to
anyone if you kill yourself—but her feet wouldn't
obey.

Dear God, where was he?

The cliff was getting steeper. She pushed herself harder, clambering, clinging, calling.

She paused on a tiny ledge, forcing herself to take a second to work out the best way to proceed, to look down, search…

And she saw him—well, his blue hoodie… He was a kid, sprawled among the rocks and mud by the river bank.

Not buried.

'Pete,' she screamed, and he raised his arm in a feeble wave.

Not dead. Not dead.

She choked back a sob and stepped off her ledge, heading straight for him.

The ground gave way under her.

She lurched and flailed for something to hold onto.

Everything was moving. She was sliding…the whole world was sliding.

'Pete,' she yelled again, uselessly, and then even more uselessly, 'Blake…'

And then a rock rose up to meet her and there was nothing.

Blake hadn't known he could drive so fast. He hadn't known he could be so afraid.

He hauled his car to a halt beside Maggie's, beside Tom's upturned wreck, and he was beside the shaking Tom almost before the car stopped.

'Maggie?'

'Pete's down there somewhere,' Tom said, pointing uselessly downward. Sobbing. 'An' Maggie went after him. Only then the rocks fell and I heard Maggie scream and there's been nothing since.'

CHAPTER TEN

MAGGIE woke up to whiteness—and to the worst headache she'd ever known.

It was blowing her head away. It was making her feel…

A bowl was right where she needed it, strong hands were holding her steady, and there was a voice…

'It's okay, love. It'll pass soon. We've got you safe. We're getting you stronger pain relief.'

Blake.

She was too weak to ask questions. She was too busy concentrating on the dictates of her stomach, but between spasms…

Blake?

White. Blake. Alive.

The spasms eased. The bowl was removed and Blake's hands, strong and gentle at the same time, guided her back to the pillows. Someone in green…someone at the periphery of her vision… was giving her an injection.

She got that. One arm was having an injection. Blake had the other. It was Blake's hand.

What…? What…?

'Pete…' Somehow she managed to whisper it, but inside the word was a scream.

'Pete's copped a broken leg and a dislocated shoulder,' Blake told her. 'He's had surgery and he's in the next ward. He's fine.'

In the next ward. It was so hard thinking through the fuzz. Ward. Hospital.

Blake.

Kids.

Panic.

'I have to go home.'

'You don't have to go anywhere,' he said gently. 'Ronnie's at home with the kids. They're ringing in every hour to see how you are. They all send their love. They're fine, my love. Close your eyes until the pain eases.'

It was good advice, she decided. It was advice she needed to take. The pain in her head…

She lay back and let the pain take her. She gave in to it, rode it, figured she could live with it if only she stayed absolutely still and didn't let the light in.

'Her pulse is settling,' someone said from a long way away. 'Are you sure about transfer?'

'We can do without it.' That was Blake again.

'Ross concurs. The pressure's not building and she's conscious. She'll want to stay home.'

Home.

Blake.

Kids.

He'd answered all her questions.

His hand was still holding hers and she wasn't letting go. It was helping her ride the pain. She held onto his hand, and it helped.

The waves were receding a bit. A lot? A fog was taking its place—infinitely preferable. She drifted into it, but she still didn't let go of that hand.

'Let yourself sleep,' Blake said, and his voice was right by her ear. She could feel him breathing. She could feel the faint rasp of stubble of his face against hers.

Blake. Here. Good.

Why?

'What…?'

'You hit your head,' he told her. 'Hard. We had to drill a wee hole to ease the pressure.'

'Dr Samford did,' another voice said. A woman. She dared a glimpse and saw the green again as the voice went on. 'He operated on you, down in all that mud and slush. Relieved the pressure before it killed you. How he ever managed it… It doesn't bear thinking about. Everyone's talking about it. Maggie, you're so lucky.'

It was Mary, Maggie thought. With the pain receding it was easier—but not as easy as all that— to think. To figure things out. To realise she knew this voice in green. It was Mary Walford, Theatre Nurse at Corella Base Hospital

Falling. Pete.

Drill a wee hole…

Pressure.

'A…a cranial burr-hole?' Her voice was hardly a whisper.

'A beautiful, successful drill. Ross Myers helped clean it up when we got you here,' Mary said. 'But Blake did the urgent stuff. He's quite some hero. Now sleep, Maggie, love.'

'Blake…'

'I'm going nowhere,' Blake said, in a voice that was so unsteady she hardly recognised it. His hold on her hand didn't ease one bit. 'Sleep as long as you like. I'll be here when you wake up.'

She slept and woke and slept and woke and every time she woke he was with her. He seemed to be drifting in and out of her fog. Holding her. Telling things were okay. His hand was her link to reality. Otherwise she'd float, she thought. Disappear.

Every now and then the pain would rise and she'd need that hand even more. Then there'd be a growl from Blake and movement and people and the fog would descend again.

And his hand kept right on holding her. Stopping her disappearing into the whiteness.

He was her one reality, she thought with the only vestige of reality she had left to her. Blake.

'Sleep,' he kept saying whenever she stirred, whenever things started crowding in. 'There's nothing to worry about. There's nothing to do, my Maggie, except sleep.'

And finally, finally, the fog receded and she woke up. She could hardly explain it. One minute the fog was all-enveloping; the next she was opening her eyes and the fog was gone. The sun was shining on the white coverlet.

Blake was asleep in the chair beside her.

He looked appalling. He looked battle worn, unshaved, gaunt, exhausted. He looked like he should be in this bed instead of her.

His hand still held hers.

She looked down at it, at the lean, long fingers, at the strength, at the link.

She glanced out the window and saw sunshine. Water glistening—the river beyond. No rain.

She turned again to look at that hand, and Blake was wide awake and watching her.

'Good morning, sleepyhead,' he said, and smiled, but his smile was different from any smile she'd ever seen. A warrior after battle. A warrior who'd been too close…

'Sleepyhead yourself,' she whispered. 'You're the one who was sleeping.' She glanced out the window again. 'It's morning.'

'It is.'

'I've been in here all night?'

'You've been in here for two days and three nights,' he said, and waited for that to sink in.

There was a bandage on her head. She put a hand up and touched it. Felt the lack of hair.

'We had to cut it,' he said ruefully. 'I was in a bit of a hurry and I'm not much at hairdressing. When the bandages come off we'll find you a stylist.'

'I'll be punk for a while?'

'Maybe you will,' he agreed. 'Lopsided mohawk. It had to be done. You gave yourself one hell of a bang.'

She lay back on the pillows and thought about it. Blake let her hand go, poured two glasses of water, handed one to her—watched to make sure her shaking hand wasn't about to drop it—and then drank himself. He looked like a man who needed it.

Cranial burr-hole. The words came floating out of the fog. Pressure.

'You operated.'

'I was…lucky,' he said. 'You had a massive haematoma, and I could see you slipping, but Tom was driving his dad's farm ute. It had a toolbox in the back containing a drill, plus a set of lovely, new, clean drill bits. All sizes. Tom had his phone. I rang a neurologist mate in Melbourne. Tom held the phone while I drilled. Thankfully it took the pressure off instantly. Exciting, huh?'

And she heard his voice shake. She heard the lingering terror in it.

She'd seen burr-holes drilled with patients in nice, clean theatre settings, and they were so often too late.

Pressure from bleeding on the brain…

She touched the bandage again and she knew how lucky she'd been.

'Thank you,' she said simply, and he sat again and took her hand and held.

'I never knew how much I needed you,' he said simply. 'Until I thought I was losing you. I've known you for two weeks. I can't possibly need you that much but I do.'

'Blake…' He'd taken her breath away. She lay on the pillows and watched his face, and saw raw, naked need. Pain.

'Blake,' she said again, and reached out, and he moved, gathering her into his arms, gently, tenderly, holding her as she needed to be held. His heart against hers. Washing away the last of the fog. Just holding.

'I need you to marry me, Maggie,' he whispered, and her world stilled.

Marry…

He pulled away at that, and saw her face, and he laughed, a raw, jagged laugh that contained pain as well as humour.

'Um…let's recall that,' he said, and she saw he was striving for normality, for a place that didn't encompass the fear he'd faced. 'It's way too soon.'

'I…I can't…' The fog was wisping in again. All she wanted to do was say yes, sink into this man's arms and never let go, but some vestige of the old Maggie was resurfacing, ringing warning bells, stopping her from take this amazing, irreversible leap. 'Blake, I can't…think.'

'No,' he said, and he smiled and then he tugged her back to him and he kissed her, a whisper kiss, light, loving on her lips. And then he propelled her back on the pillows. 'Of course you can't. And I can't either, my love. I've hardly slept. You're full of analgesics. We need to sort ourselves out and find some sort of normality and go from there.'

He smiled at her then, and it was a smile that made her heart turn over. It was a smile that had her forgetting that her head was starting to pound again. It was a smile that made her world shift.

'I'll ring for some more pain relief for you,' he said. 'And then I'll go and wash and sleep. But then I'll come back. But I'll keep coming back, my Maggie. For now and for always, and that's a promise.'

* * *

He left. She slept and when she woke up he wasn't there. Mary was, fussing in the background, adjusting drips.

'Hi,' she said, and grinned. 'Welcome back to the real world.'

'Blake?' She couldn't help himself.

'Sent home with a flea in his ear,' she said. 'Ross told him unless he got out of here he'd get Security to eject him. He didn't want two patients and the man's exhausted. He hardly left you for three days.'

'Three days...'

'Oh, he's gorgeous,' Ronnie said happily. 'And his little girl... We brought her in here, you know, while you were so sick, because Ronnie knew he was torn. Ross decided another helicopter trip was worth it to collect her. She's a darling. Half the hospital's in love with her. But, oh, Maggie, Blake's wonderful. What a wonderful solution. You should see him with Pete. Pete's been beside himself, so scared for you, and every time you were deeply asleep Blake'd go to him. We'll wheel him in to see you later, but Blake's reassured him completely.

'Oh, he's lovely... He can be big brother to your tribe—a dad almost—and you can be mum for Ruby. Ross is already talking to him about part-time work here. Apparently he could work here two days, and Sydney three days. It's a happy ever after. The whole valley's happy for you, Maggie. It's a happy ever after for everyone.'

It took her a few more days before she felt anywhere approaching normal. She had more grazes and scrapes than she wanted to think about. She had broken ribs. She was being loaded with antibiotics and care and demands for rest, and she was being told over and over that she was the luckiest woman in the world.

She was.

She lay back on her hospital pillows, she watched the sunbeams on the coverlet, she watched the faces of her scared siblings when they visited— apparently they'd finally managed to set up a barge for river crossings. She listened to Pete's stammering apology, she hugged him, she smiled at Blake, and she watched with love as he played with Ruby on her coverlet.

Then, on the day she was due to leave hospital, she told him she wasn't going to marry him.

He'd come in by himself. The kids had pleaded to be allowed to help bring her home but that'd mean four kids and a baby. Pete's leg was in a cast so he'd need the entire back seat. It was all or none so he decreed none.

He drove to the hospital using the freshly or-

ganised barge, set in place until the bridge could
be rebuilt. The worst of the bad weather was gone.
The river level was dropping every day, only the
mass of debris on the banks showing the maelstrom it had been.

Blake wasn't looking at scenery, however. He
knew this would be decision day, and he walked
into Maggie's room and he knew the moment he
saw her face what her answer would be.

'Too soon?' he asked, trying to keep the tone
light. Trying to ignore the lurch in the pit of his
gut.

She was dressed, ready to leave with him. She
was wearing her faded jeans and a loose, over-
sized windcheater that was easy to take on and
off over her bandaged head.

She was still heavily bandaged. The Corella
Valley hairdresser had come in and clipped her
lovely curls on the undamaged parts of her scalp
back to a boyish, elfin crop.

She looked absurdly young, absurdly vulnerable—and absurdly beautiful. All he wanted to
do was gather her into his arms, yet her expression said don't.

'I can't,' she said, and her words were an-
guished.

'No,' he said. He crossed to the bed where she
was sitting and because he couldn't help himself
he tilted her chin with his fingers and brushed her

lips with his. He wanted—more than anything he'd ever wanted in his life—to gather her into his arms and kiss her as he needed to kiss her, but somehow he held back. Somehow he held to the last vestiges of his self-control.

'I can't marry you,' she whispered.

'That's what I thought you meant.'

'Blake, I'm sorry.'

'Don't be,' he said, still striving for lightness. 'It's your life, Maggie.'

'But it's not my life,' she said, and suddenly she wasn't whispering any more.

He stilled. 'Is that why?' he said slowly. 'Because you're encumbered with the kids, with responsibilities? You know I how much I want to share those.'

'That's just it,' she said bitterly. 'Of course you do.'

She turned and looked out the window. The river was flowing peacefully in the distance. From here they could see the far side of the valley. They could almost see the homestead, filled with kids and dogs and…family.

'It's my dream,' she said.

'Your drink-can dream?'

'Don't laugh.'

'I'm not laughing. I would never laugh at you.'

She turned then and met his gaze straight on. She gazed at him and he didn't falter. He looked back at her, calm and sure, and he tried to put every ounce of love he felt for this woman into that gaze.

'I know you wouldn't,' she said at last. 'I know. But it still is a dream, and if I married you…' She hesitated, touched the bandages on her head as if they hurt—but maybe it was something else that was hurting.

'Blake, these last weeks have been…stunning. For both of us. You've taken responsibility for your sister's baby. You've been immersed in my family up to your ears. You've been hauled out of your life as an independent city surgeon, engaged—all right,' she added hastily as she saw his face—'partnered by a colleague you've been with for years. You've come back to a place that's filled with emotion for you and I've thrown more at you. You've saved my brother's life and you've saved mine.

'That's an awesome amount of emotion to jam into three weeks. Do you think I should ask you to commit for the rest of your life on the strength of it? It's been a crazy, roller-coaster ride, Blake. Now you need to get off the roller-coaster, settle, figure where you want to take things with Ruby and go from there.'

'I need you, Maggie,' he said, surely and steadily. 'Yes, it's only three weeks but when I thought I could lose you…' He broke off and he knew she could hear the power of what he'd gone through.

At the base of a cliff. Watching the swelling…

It still made him feel ill, but it wasn't helping his cause.

'I never knew what love was,' he said simply. 'Until I thought I'd lost you. If love is needing, like needing a part of me…'

'But I'm not needful, Blake,' she said, calmly and steadily. 'I'm grateful—you can't imagine how grateful I am, but I won't marry you because I need you. Even if…even if your need is love. I've fallen for you, hard, but I'm seeing you as a guy who's taken on his baby niece, who helped me save Christopher and Pete, who saved me. And, yes, who needs me. But that's not a basis for a marriage.'

'No, but love is. Surely the two combine. Maggie, I've thought it out. We could organise things… I could work a couple of days in Sydney a week and spend the rest of the time here. We could fill the house with kids. They could come and go as they pleased, back and forth to your mother, back and forth to us. You'd be there whenever they need you. Ruby would have a mother…'

It was the wrong thing to say. He knew it as he saw her expression change. He had this all wrong.

This was not a sure and loving Maggie. This was still a trapped Maggie.

'I would be,' she whispered. 'Ruby's twisting herself around my heart already. But it's not fair.'

'Fair?'

'My heart's already so twisted,' she said. 'From the time I can first remember. "Maggie, push your brother's pram, he's crying. Maggie, your little sister's wet. Maggie, sleep with Liseile, she's having nightmares. Maggie, you need to stay home from school this week, Donny's got measles." And I did it. Every single time, I did it—how could I not? Because I loved them. I love them. And here you are, asking me to love…more.'

'You don't want…'

'Of course I want,' she said, and she tilted her chin and looked at him—really looked at him. 'I'm falling so hard. If you took me into your arms right now…' But she put up her hands as if to ward him off. 'But I don't want you to.

'Really?

'I don't know,' she said, and she didn't sound sure any more. She sounded…scared. Desolate. 'Blake, I don't know. All I do know is that I'm not game to try. I'd marry you and it'd be gorgeous and the whole valley would be happy for me. The kids would be beside themselves and it'd solve all your problems and I'd end up loving Ruby to bits… And one day I might wake up and think, What did I collect all those tin cans for?'

'We could travel,' he said, slowly, trying to

sound confident. Trying to sound like he thought her qualms were minor. 'Together.'

'But I've had...*together*,' she said, and she flinched as she said it. 'I know. That sounds appalling when I say I'm falling in love with you in the same breath, but I've never had anything but together. You've come here for three weeks, you've walked straight into my together and you think it's magic. But you've had, what, thirty-six years of You. I've never had Me and I want it. I want to learn Me.'

She shook her head then, falling silent. He watched her, quiet and still, knowing the time for argument was not now. Knowing that pushing her now would do his cause no good—would even do harm. Knowing he had to let her be.

'Blake, I'm scared,' she whispered. 'I'm terrified I'll wake up in ten years surrounded by more kids and more dogs and more drama, and I'll resent it all and become a bitter old lady who snaps at kids and locks herself in the bathroom and sulks...'

'The bathroom?' he said faintly.

'It's the only place I can ever get away,' she said. 'And even then they bang on the door. "Maggie, hurry up, I need a note for school. Maggie, I need to tell you about my boyfriend. Maggie, if this pimple doesn't go down I'll die." And don't you dare laugh, Blake Samford.'

'I won't laugh. I've told you before, I'd never laugh at you, Maggie.'

'And don't be gorgeous either,' she managed, trying to glare, only her eyes were filling. She swiped away tears with anger and the desire to gather her in his arms was overwhelming. He didn't. He was proud of himself that he didn't, but it nearly killed him.

'So, what,' he said at last. 'Back to the seven-year plan, huh?'

'I… Yes,' she said. 'It's better than nothing.'

'I'm better than nothing.'

'Yes, you are,' she said, controlling herself again. Taking a deep breath and moving on. 'But you deserve something more than a woman who's scared that marriage might seem a trap.'

'I'd never marry you if you felt like that.'

'Well, then,' she said, and rose and looked down at her packed duffel bag. At her hospital room crowded with flowers from almost everyone in the valley. At him.

'Well, then,' she said again. 'It's time to go home. Time for you to go back to Sydney. Time for me to find another place to live.

'I'm not selling the farm, Maggie.'

'You're not?'

'There's not a thing you can do about that,' he told her. 'I've fallen for the farm as well.'

'You're not…going to live there?'

'No,' he said. 'I wouldn't do that to myself. To live next door to you…'

'You'll take Ruby back to Sydney?'

'Yes.'

'Will you cope?'

'I believe I can,' he said, and managed a grin. 'Without calling on Maggie. But, Maggie…'

'Yes?'

'I'm not moving out of your life. Not entirely. I'm your landlord and I'll need to check the farm out from time to time. As well as that, the kids have done some heart twisting as well. I've promised Pete I'll take him to Sydney and get him some driving lessons as soon as he turns sixteen. I'd like to organise an online tutor for Liselle and her calculus.'

'There's no need—'

'There is a need,' he said softly. 'Just because you can't marry me it doesn't mean I can stop caring.'

'You…understand.'

'Yes, I do,' he said with a heavy heart, and he did. 'I wish I didn't, but I do. I wish… I wish…' He hesitated and then he shrugged. 'I'm not sure what I wish,' he told her, and he lifted her duffel with one hand and took her hand in the other. 'But let's take you home, and let's get on with our lives while I figure it out.'

CHAPTER ELEVEN

CHRISTMAS at the Tildens' was always crazy. Everyone was home, and the tiny house was bursting at the seams.

'Let's have Christmas at Blake's,' Liselle had pleaded. 'It's huge and Blake won't mind.'

He wouldn't mind, Maggie thought. He'd been a constant presence in the kids' lives for six months now and they regarded him more as a benevolent uncle than as Maggie's landlord.

He'd only visited twice, flying visits to install a new farm manager—Harold was too old and Blake didn't want Maggie responsible for his cattle—and to check for himself that Pete's leg was healing as he thought it should.

They'd been fast trips and he hadn't brought Ruby. 'I have a fabulous housekeeper-nanny,' he told Maggie. 'And I've given up the job as Head of Orthopaedics. I'm an Indian rather than a chief now, but it means I spend more time with my little girl.'

He'd brought photographs and he showed them to her with pride, but he made no mention of marriage, no mention that he wasn't coping without her, no mention that she'd made the wrong decision.

She hadn't, she told herself over and over, but the kids had his number on speed dial, she heard them chatting to him about trivial stuff, and she felt...jealous?

Ridiculous.

But he was a friend. The boys took their troubles to Blake now, and for that she was grateful.

Liselle got first-class honours in her calculus. 'Blake thinks I can be a doctor,' she'd told Maggie, almost bursting with pride. 'He's going to help me.'

Somehow he'd inveigled himself into their lives and she loved him for it.

But not enough?

Not enough to want Christmas at his house. Not enough to think she'd made a mistake.

Now she woke up on Christmas morning and for about the thousandth time since he'd left she thought of him straight away.

She was back at her mother's house. She was sharing a bed with Susie. Liselle was in the bed beside them. Blackie and Tip were under the bed. All her brothers and sisters were home.

She was surrounded, just like always. Any minute now she'd get up and stuff the turkey. Her mother would waft out for present giving and set up candles on the table or make a new cocktail. Her father might drop in later with the pregnant Sashabelle. Expecting gifts. Not giving any.

But things were easing. Donny had finished his apprenticeship and Nickie had graduated and was choosing between three excellent job offers. Two down, six to go.

Six years left?

To what? Kir on the Left Bank of Paris.

It was losing its gloss.

I'm turning sour already, she thought, and decided, Turkey. She tossed back the covers—and paused.

She'd heard a truck approaching—or trucks? They stopped, just outside the house.

As her feet touched the bare wooden floor there was an enormous whine, like the tray on a truck heaving upwards…

And then a crash that had her jumping out of her skin. That had Liselle and Susie sitting bolt upright in bed and the dogs going out of their minds.

Another crash, bigger than the first.

Amazingly Susie was giggling, whooping, heading for the door. And then she looked back as if she'd forgotten something important. She grabbed an envelope from under the pillow.

'Blake said to give you this,' she said importantly. 'But I have to get mine to put on top.' She dived under the bed and hauled out a huge plastic bag filled with…cans. Empty drink cans.

'And me,' Liselle said sleepily. 'Mine are in the wardrobe. Open it, Susie, love.'

Susie obligingly opened the wardrobe—and let loose a cascade of cans.

'They're from the whole of Corella Valley High,' Louise said proudly. 'Six months' collecting.'

The door opened. The rest of her family was crowding in the doorway.

'Here's ours,' they told her, and they were practically buried in cans.

'What…? What…?'

'I've got some, too.' It was her mother, holding two small bags of cans like they were diamonds. 'I had to change drinking bottled tonic to canned tonic, just for you, love. But it was worth it. You're a good girl, Maggie.'

'But it's mostly from Blake. It's Blake's present.' Christopher was practically bouncing with excitement. 'Come and see, come and see, come and see.'

So she went, pushing through a sea of cans, still clutching her unopened envelope.

Peter had the front door wide, and his beam was almost wider. 'How cool is this?' he demanded.

'Blake says these are from the whole of Sydney Central Hospital for six months. And it's every single person in the valley. And Donny's garage and our school and university, and Blake says we have enough for at least six months...'

'Shush,' Susie said, bossy and exasperated. 'She hasn't read the letter.'

She wasn't looking at the letter. She was looking at a mountain. Cans, cans and more cans. The entire yard was buried under drink cans.

'Two shipping containers,' Pete said, awed. 'Two full shipping containers, plus what we've got. You have no idea, Maggie...'

'Blake...' she breathed.

'Read the letter,' Susie demanded, and finally the little girl lost patience with her big sister, ripped it open, stood in front of her and read out loud.

'*"Darling Maggie..."*. Oooer, darling...'

'Cut it out,' Louise snapped. 'Read it like it is.'

Susie glowered and then grinned and read.

'*"Darling Maggie. Seven years is too long. Anything could happen in seven years. They could stop serving kir on the Left Bank. The pyramids might erode. I could wear out waiting. So here's an alternative. We've weighed our cans and we figure they're good for six months' travel. On your own. With what you already have, plus the extras the kids have found since we weighed them, we reckon you can go and see whatever you want in the world. But before you start objecting, you need to listen to the rest of the plan..."'*

'I don't need to read this,' Susie said. 'I know.'

'Blake's taking six months' leave,' Liselle said. 'It's paternity leave 'cos he's formally adopting Ruby.'

'And he's staying at Corella View,' Pete said. 'And he's going to teach me cool driving stuff.'

'And we can stay here with Mum or we can stay with him if Mum gets sick of us,' Chris added, with a sideways glance at his mother.

'And Ronnie's promised to look after Ruby if Blake starts feeling…house…house…'

'Housebound,' Louise finished for her. 'But us older ones are planning on coming home often as well. You've done so much for us, Maggie.'

'And Blake and Ronnie have organised you time off work,' Pete added.

'And Blake says he can get you a passport really fast. He says you should go to Africa first 'cos it'll be cold in Europe in winter. But he says it's up to you.'

'Blake…' she managed again.

'A million cans,' her mother said. 'All over my front lawn. I'll give him such a talking to when I see him next.'

'Which would be now,' a low voice said, and

she whirled and it was Blake. He was standing on the veranda. Watching. Listening.

He was dressed even more casually than the day she'd first seen him. Faded jeans. A checked, open-necked shirt. Boots. He looked like a farmer rather than a city surgeon.

He was holding Ruby.

Cattleman with baby?

He looked so sexy he made her toes curl.

'You're free,' he said, softly, firmly, lovingly. 'Maggie Tilden, your seven-year plan just turned into now. We've all done it. We love you, Maggie, and we're sending you away.'

'But you'll come back?' Susie asked, suddenly anxious. 'Maggie, you won't forget us? You'll come home?'

Blake was smiling at her. Smiling and smiling. Her heart was turning somersaults, backward flips, any gymnastic manoeuvre it could think of. All at once.

She wished she wasn't wearing pyjamas. She wished she wasn't surrounded by family. She wished she wasn't surrounded by thousands of tin cans.

No, she didn't. She wished for none of those things because for now, for this moment, there was only this man, only this moment, this smile.

Blake.

'You did all this,' she managed.

'Six months' scrounging,' he said, and chuckled. 'I owe favours to every janitor in Sydney.'

'The kids…'

'Scrounged like champions. See, we all want to get rid of you. Mostly because we figure…if we set you free, you'll fly home.'

'Like a pigeon.'

'I prefer dove,' he said comfortably. 'A lovely, loving white dove. Liselle, do you think you might take Ruby for a moment? I can't see any mistletoe but I'm sure there's some around here somewhere. I need to kiss your sister goodbye.'

'Goodbye…'

'With no promises,' he said, as he headed along the veranda to where she was standing, barefooted in her pyjamas, tousled with sleep. As he gathered her into his arms and held her. Just held her. Asking for no promises. Placing no expectations on her.

'We're giving you yourself back, Maggie, love,' he told her. 'We're giving you the world in the shape of a mountain of tin cans. And if you can see your way to steering this way at the end of your adventures…'

'Kiss her now,' Donny yelled. 'Go on, mate, get it over with.'

'No pressure,' Blake said, and his dark eyes gleamed down into hers. 'No pressure, Maggie, love, but if you could possibly tilt your chin…'

She did. How could a girl not?

How could a woman not kiss a man who was giving her the world?

Who wasn't asking her to marry him.

Who was setting her free.

She watched giraffes sway majestically across the African savannah. She woke under canvas and in the dawn she heard lions roaring. She had to shoo monkeys from her breakfast. She wrote to Blake about it.

He sent photos back of Ruby and told her how his work was going and talked to her about a new breed of cattle he thought he might introduce to the farm.

She took camel rides around the pyramids. A kid photographed her for money and she emailed the snap home.

Blake sent a snap of himself riding a horse he'd bought. It seemed Liselle was teaching him how to ride.

She watched funeral pyres beside the Ganges and wondered how she could describe the smell, the sights to Blake. She wandered from street stall to street stall and she didn't get sick once. Blake sounded almost irritated. 'Everyone gets sick— what's your stomach made of?'

He sent advice on hygiene and links to sites on intestinal worms. She laughed but he also sent a picture of him at a staff dinner at Corella Hospital and she looked at Mary standing beside him and she thought…she thought…

No. She wouldn't think. She was free.

She walked the Great Wall in China—okay, not all of it but enough to get sore feet—and she gazed at the hidden warriors with awe and gratitude that she could be in this place at this time.

Blake had seen them, too. She wished…

No, she couldn't wish, for who could wish for more than she'd dreamed of?

She drank Guinness in fabulous Irish pubs. She checked out some ancestors and decided she liked being a little bit Irish.

Blake told her about how Mary had been to Ireland last year and researched all her Irish ancestors.

She was interested—sort of. She liked Mary. Mary was a friend.

Why the niggle?

She dived from a caique into the turquoise waters off a Greek isle. She got sunburned, but she didn't tell Blake because he'd lecture her and she liked being free to get sunburned or not. Didn't she?

She wandered the bazaars in Istanbul, Cairo, Morocco. She looked, she tasted, she smelled and she listened. She drank kir on the Left Bank in

Paris. She looked and looked and looked and she felt and felt and felt.

And she tried not to wish for more.

Every night she went back to her hotel room or her tent or yurt, or whatever weird and wonderful place she was staying in and she used the fantastic satellite internet Blake had organised for her and she contacted home.

She told the kids what she'd done that day. Sometimes they were interested. Mostly they were more interested in telling her the things that were happening to them.

And almost every night she talked to Blake, who was interested in her. Who asked the right questions. Who got it that she'd been disappointed in kir. Who grinned when she said the Eiffel tower was just too high and she'd taken the lift. Who agreed that seal colonies stank.

Who showed her pictures of a happy, bouncing, healing Ruby with pride, who explained that her legs were almost in line now, and she was sitting up, and teething. Who talked about the valley with love and with pride. Who spoke of the people he was meeting, of Ronnie, who was awesome at helping, and Mary, who was such a friend…

He smiled at her and said goodnight—even when it was morning his time—and he sent her to sleep happy. Or happyish. For the longer she was away, the more she thought. She was living a dream but what if, in following her dream, she was letting another go?

What if she'd made a mistake?

She hadn't. She knew she'd made the right decision. She loved what she was doing and she embraced it with all her heart, but the heart swelled to fit all comers and there was a corner...a Blake corner...

Please, her heart whispered. Please...

And six months later she walked through the customs gates at Sydney airport, feeling jet-lagged, feeling weird, feeling hopeful but almost afraid to hope...

Blake was there.

All by himself.

No kids. No Ruby.

No Mary.

Just Blake.

'My love,' he said as she reached him, and he held out his arms.

She walked right into them. He folded her against his heart, and she stayed there for a very long time.

He'd organised things so Ronnie was with Ruby, so they had the night in Sydney to themselves.

He took her back to his new little bachelor-nursery pad near the hospital and he made her dinner while she spent half an hour under streaming-hot water and washed every part of her. She dressed in jogging pants and a windcheater because she had nothing else clean. Most of her luggage was still in the back of Blake's car, ready to be taken to Corella Valley the next day. She'd kept only her overnight bag. She should have kept something special aside, she thought ruefully. A little black dress?

A sexy negligee?

But she walked out of the bathroom and Blake was stirring something at the stove. He was wearing jeans and an apron. He turned and smiled at her and his smile said it didn't matter one whit what she was wearing. She could be wearing nothing.

She loved this man with all her heart. She'd loved this man around the world and back again— and she'd come home.

'Will you marry me now?' he asked, and her world stood still.

'I think I might just have stuffed that,' he said ruefully as the silence stretched on. 'Patience is not my strong suit. I thought…dinner. Champagne. Something romantic playing in the background. It's just… I look at you and I can't…'

He stopped. He took off his apron. He took the eight steps that separated them and took her hands in his.

'I got it wrong,' he told her. 'I've had months

to think about it, almost a year, and I know exactly how I got it wrong. I told you I needed you. Maybe I do; maybe that's part of the equation, but it's not the main thing here. The main thing, the huge, overriding elephant in the room, or more than elephant if I can think of anything bigger, is that I love you, Maggie Tilden. I've loved you since the first moment I saw you. So…can you cope without the violins and roses? Can we look past the need? Can you forget that I ever needed you and can you just love me?'

And how was a woman to answer that?

With an open heart.

'I…I always have,' she whispered. And then, more firmly, because the joy in her heart was settling, fitting into all the edges with a sweetness that made the path ahead seem sure and true and right, 'My love, I always will.'

And they looked at each other, just looked, and something passed between them, so sweet, so strong that Maggie knew a bond was forged right then that would last for ever.

'I'm not asking you to be mother to Ruby,' he said. 'I've organised—'

'Hush,' she told him, and she placed her finger on his lips. 'I'm not asking you to be a brother to my siblings either, but I have a feeling you already are. And Ruby's as much mine as yours. If you're willing to share.'

'Maggie, to ask you to take us on…'

'I don't think it's taking on,' she managed. 'It's loving. It's different.'

'Six months ago…'

'I wasn't where I am now,' she said, steadily, lovingly, because she'd had six months to think this through and every night as she'd talked to Blake she'd become more and more sure of where her heart lay.

'I've been surrounded by love since I was born. Trapped by it, in a sense. What you've done for me, Blake…you've set me free so I can choose love. I've had six wonderful months of being by myself, but I wasn't by myself. I had the kids in the background. I had Ruby. I had Corella Valley. They were my rock, my base, my knowledge that of all the places in the world, there was a place for me. But most of all there was you. My one true thing. My love.'

'Maggie…' He held her, tenderly though, as if she was fragile. As if she might evaporate. As if she might still gather her things and head out that door, back to the world. 'Maggie, are you sure?'

'I've never been more sure,' she whispered.

'I've organised it. I've cut back, hard. I'm a part-time doctor until Ruby reaches school age. She's my responsibility, Maggie, not yours.'

'I'll be a part-time nurse, too,' she said comfortably. 'If you don't mind sharing.'

'Maggie…'

She pulled back and looked at him—really looked at him. Needing him to see the whole package. 'I still need to stay in Corella Valley,' she said.

'Of course you do,' he said. 'Just lucky there's a fabulous homestead and enough work for both of us. I'm getting on brilliantly with the hospital staff—they've called on me already, and you should see the new bridge!'

'You'd stay there?'

'The Valley needs an orthopaedic surgeon. It also needs a fabulous district nurse-cum-midwife. How lucky's that?'

'Lucky?' she whispered. 'Or meant?'

'I guess meant,' he said as he tilted her chin and gazed into her eyes. 'Maggie, I've loved you to the ends of the earth and back and I always will, but now will you come home with me?'

'I… Something's burning on the stove.' How had she noticed that when all she could feel was him?

'Maggie…'

'Yes, I will,' she said, positively, absolutely, and she wrapped her arms around this man she loved with all her heart. Who cared if the apartment burned—this was more important. 'I may travel again but it'll take ages to collect enough cans.

Double this time because wherever I go, you go. Plus Ruby. Plus whoever else needs us.'

'That's a lot of can collecting,' he said unsteadily. 'I wonder if champagne bottles count.'

'I'm sure they do.' The smell was getting stronger. Maybe she could be practical Maggie for a moment. 'Blake, the dinner…'

'I s'pose,' he said, and sighed dramatically and swept her up into his arms and held her close. Two strides took him to the cooker and the gas was turned off.

'Disaster averted,' he told her. 'But I'm not thinking dinner right now.' He was carrying her towards the bedroom, laughing down at her, loving her with his eyes. 'So, Maggie Tilden, love of my life, woman of my dreams, will you marry me? Will you take me on as well as all the other wonderful loves you hold in your heart?'

'You're the biggest,' she said, and she smiled back at him. She smiled and smiled, at this lovely, sexy, toe-curlingly gorgeous man who promised to be a part of her life for ever. 'You're the biggest and the best, and you're my for-ever love. Of course I'll marry you.'

And then they reached the bedroom and there was nothing else to say.

Two people were one.

They were Maggie and Blake, and they were starting their whole life together.

* * *

And in Corella Valley…

'I've got two hundred and three,' Susie announced, looking at her pile of cans with satisfaction.

'I'm up to four hundred and sixty,' Chris crowed. 'And Liselle says her dorm's up to a thousand. How many do you reckon before we can all go?'

'I'm guessing trillions but we can do it. Maggie'll be so happy.'

'Maggie *and* Blake,' Chris corrected her. 'But you're right. Gee, it's going to take a lot of cans for all of us.'

'We've got time,' Susie said in satisfaction. 'If we just keep collecting and collecting we'll be able to do anything we want. Do you reckon they'll mind that we've filled Maggie's bedroom with cans as a homecoming present?'

'Nah,' Chris said. 'They've got loads of bedrooms. I reckon they'll only want one from now on.'

'Really?'

'Yeah,' Chris said with thirteen-year-old wisdom. 'I think Maggie's given up being alone.'

* * * * *